Silver Moon

Hot Moon Rising Book 6

By
Merryn Dexter

~A Note from the Author~

I am so pleased to be working again with the amazing Decadent Publishing team – dreams really do come true! My imagination is fired up so I hope to be able to bring you many more stories in partnership with them.

I would be thrilled to hear from you about this book, Hot Moon Rising, Wiccan Haus, the Black Hills Wolves, soup recipes, holidays, or anything else that crosses your mind. I'm a military spouse currently resident in Belgium and working from home so always happy for a distraction!

You can email me at merryn.dexter@yahoo.com or find me on Facebook or Twitter @MerrynDexter . I also have a website www.merryndexter.com and a blog www.merryndexter.blogspot.be

Best Wishes
Merryn x

Dedication

For M. Who brings a little bit of magic into my life every day.

Moonlight Wolf Pack

Charlie Aquino (human) – Detective for the sheriff's gang task force for Palmetto County Sheriff's Department. His partner is Jesse Farrell.
- Mate: Liana Cosa

Liana Cosa Aquino – Refugee from a different pack. She works part-time as a waitress at Moonlight Diner.
- Mate: Charlie Aquino

Silver Ellis (human) – Was the witness of a violent crime and placed in Kirk's protection as a favor to Jesse Farrell and Charlie Aquino. Works as a school teacher.
- Mate: Kirk Matheson

Alexa Martin Farrell – Left her pack over a disagreement with her alpha. She moved to Florida and helped the pack find a small community of cottages in Moonlight, Florida. She works as an Internet researcher and gets jobs through her online website. She also does research for The Defenders.
- Mate: Jesse Farrell

Jesse Farrell (human) – Detective for the sheriff's gang task force for Palmetto County Sheriff's Department. His partner is Charlie Aquino.
- Mate: Alexa Martin (who saved him when on assignment he was attacked by a gang)

Riesa Marlowe (human) – A psychic who helped locate Hannah Raines.
- Mate: Derek Sawyer

Kirk Matheson – Works for The Defenders Agency. Has a cabin offset in the woods, about a mile from town.
- Mate: Silver Ellis

Hannah Raines Molina – She was kidnapped and saved by Jesse and Charlie with the help of Riesa Marlowe, a psychic. Works as Alexa Martin's research assistant.
- Mate: Rand Molina

Rand Molina - Derek's second-in-command in the Moonlight pack. Partners with Derek Sawyer at The Defenders, a private security agency.
- Mate: Hannah Raines

Derek Sawyer – Alpha of a small pack. Most of their original clan was destroyed when developers took the land they were living on and many of their pack were killed by hunters. They hid in an abandoned orange grove until Alexa offered them the bungalows in exchange for their help. He and the others have embraced Jesse and Alexa and Charlie and Liana and given the female shifters a new sense of belonging.
- Partners with Rand Molina at The Defenders Agency, a private security and bodyguard agency.
- Mate: Riesa Marlowe

Alan Shifflett - When shifted, Alan appears with snaggled teeth and missing patches of hair. He's prone to violent outbursts. His teeth tear his lips, leaving wounds when he shifts. His father owns Moonlight Diner, which he is currently managing. He is also a programmer.
- Mate: Shelley Fields

The Defenders Agency - A private security and bodyguard agency formed by Rand and Derek once they were established in the little enclave of cottages. It provides good income for the pack. A majority of the pack is involved in the cases they take.
Jesse and Charlie are their contacts with the sheriff's department and also refer many cases to them.

Chapter One

Silver Ellis studied the lowered heads of her class bent over the math test she had set for them. The empty space in the second row gnawed at her. *Where is Tina?* Today marked the fourth day she'd missed class in the past fortnight. A disturbing new trend from one of her brightest and most promising students. Tina loved school. Soaked up every bit of new knowledge like an eager sponge. She was a bright spot in Silver's otherwise disappointing experience at Johnson Middle School. Moving had proved a mistake—an instinctive response to the blinding grief of losing her father.

Six months. I said I would give it six months. The lie sat heavy in her gut. She'd been there for three months and knew, once the semester finished, she would move on. Her quiet existence hadn't prepared Silver for the shocking poverty and gang violence overshadowing the area.

Her dreams of making a difference to the local children dissolved in the face of harsh reality. She was a stranger, a naïve fool raised in relative comfort, and the quiet security of a small town. She knew nothing about the struggles these children faced even to make it to class. Absent parents, tight budgets, and poor welfare support. Younger siblings that needed minding while their mothers staggered between a series of underpaid manual jobs, trying to scrape together enough money to keep corrupt landlords at bay.

The children in her class ranged from hollow-eyed disinterest to belligerent defiance. Tina's natural enthusiasm rubbed off on a couple of them, but most barely tolerated Miss Ellis with her old-fashioned skirts, pussy-cat bow blouses, and sensible shoes.

"One more minute, finish up what you're writing," she called out to a chorus of sighs and muttered curses. The level of profanity peppering everyday exchanges with her group of ten year olds still stunned her. She'd taken to writing down some of the more outlandish insults in her notebook. An online urban dictionary had proved most enlightening—and disturbing. "And that's time. Don't forget to write your names on the top of your test papers and place them on the corner of my desk on your way out."

The bell rang, signaling the end of class. Chairs scraped back and the students formed a mini stampede toward freedom, tossing their papers haphazardly on her desk as they passed. Bending to gather a few stray pages from the floor, Silver raised her eyes when a pair of battered tennis shoes stopped in front of her. Suppressing a qualm of fear, she met the fierce glare of her most recalcitrant student. Nina would be the star of every subject if she ever bothered to apply her considerable intelligence. Silver didn't know what had happened to the girl to make her so bitter—didn't want to know if she was completely honest with herself. *Coward.*

"What is it, Nina?" Silver smiled in encouragement. A tiny frisson of hope skittered through her nervousness. Maybe the girl actually had a question about the test.

"Why the fuck do you keep bothering with this crap? Math isn't gonna help any of these stupid-ass fools." Rage glittered in the girl's dark eyes. Silver pushed quickly to her feet, not wishing to present such a vulnerable target.

"Math is vital to every aspect of life, Nina. A good education can open a world of opportunity to you. You have so much ability, there is no reason you couldn't go to college when the time comes; you just need to apply yourself a little." Silver couldn't help the pleading tone in her voice. She wanted so much to help.

"Education didn't do you no good. How else did you end up in this shithole place? School is a waste of time. I know what my options are for making money, and a fancy college diploma won't help me." The girl leaned forward, making Silver shrink back from the fury shaking her too-thin frame. "Don't need a diploma to turn tricks," she hissed through clenched teeth. "Don't need a diploma to get in good with a banger."

Tears thickened in Silver's throat. Ten years old and this child was already so certain her worth would only ever be counted in sexual terms. "Nina, oh honey...." The sympathetic hand she extended was slapped away, the sting nothing in comparison to the pain in her heart.

"Don't. Don't you pity me, bitch!" A fleck of

spittle gathered at the corner of the girl's lips. "You don't belong here. Take that prissy-ass attitude of yours somewhere else." Nina spun on her heel and stormed from the room, leaving an oppressive cloud of anger in her wake.

Silver sank into her chair, staring at the crumpled test papers in her hand. Doodles, elaborately decorated curse words, and a few scribbled answers stared back at her. *What the hell am I doing here?*

A soft knock disturbed her pity party, and she glanced over at the fierce-looking woman leaning against the doorframe. Marney Williams adjusted the huge, battered purse over her shoulder and tapped her wrist. "Come on, girl. It's twofers at Joe's Tavern and you look even more in need of a bellyful of cocktails than I do."

Silver studied the pile of tests on her desk, the words of refusal dying on her lips. No one would care whether the tests were marked, apart from her. She didn't drink on a school night, one of the many rules she'd set herself. She'd didn't exactly knock the booze back on the weekends either, though. Didn't do much of anything really since her father passed the previous year, leaving her rattling around the house on her own. Spreading her wings, moving on, and starting a new life had been the plan. Instead, she stayed home in her little apartment, living vicariously through the books she read and the shows on her television. Marney clutched her throat, making exaggerated noises until Silver shook her head and stuffed the folded test papers in the large rucksack she used as her work bag.

Grabbing her sensible black overcoat from

behind the door, she hurried down the corridor in the wake of the other teacher's clacking high-heeled boots. The oversized cream sweater Marney wore slid down, revealing a shapely mocha-colored shoulder. Her painted-on jeans were tucked into black leather boots. Silver tugged her coat closer over her long tweed skirt and high-necked blouse. The flat heels of the lace-up shoes clumped on the tiled floor. *Twenty-five going on fifty-five.* Shrugging off the unflattering self-comparison with her colleague, Silver rushed to catch up with her friend. Maybe if she spent a bit more of her free time in the company of the confident woman, instead of holed-up in her little apartment, some of Marney's style might rub off on her. She tried to picture her plump little body poured into tight denim and winced. *Maybe not.*

***

The bar was busy, the post-work crowd sucking back beers and cocktails in an attempt to wash away the trials of the day in alcohol's soothing embrace. Silver sipped the sickly-sweet concoction in front of her and forced a smile at the boorish man crammed too close onto the seat next to her. The high-backed booth hemmed them in, offering little hope of escape from his attentions. Marney cooed and flirted with his much better-looking friend on the opposite side of the table. She'd begun to suspect her colleague had an ulterior motive for inviting her the moment she made a beeline for the two men. Sitting down first had been a big mistake. Her repeated attempts to shuffle away from Pete, her date, were now thwarted by the wall. Fingers brushed her shoulder again, and she sat forward, shrugging off his unwelcome touch. His hand moved from her shoulder to her hair, bound at the base of her neck in a thick bun. He yanked the thick band holding it in place, and she winced in pain when the elastic caught in the thick mass. She slapped him away then gathered the glossy, brown length and knotted it up before it could cascade down her back.

"Relax, baby. You've hardly touched your drink," Pete slurred, blowing whisky fumes against her cheek. He'd already knocked back several beers, each with a chaser, and a faint sheen of sweat speckled his receding hairline.

"I'm fine," she gritted out, crossing her legs to avoid the hand wandering toward her thigh.

"Jeez, you're a cold fish," he muttered, pushing out of the booth to weave unsteadily toward the bar.

Leaping at the chance to escape, Silver stood up and pulled on her coat. Marney stopped flirting with her date long enough to frown at her. "Where are you going, Silver?"

"I've got some work to do; thanks for a nice evening." The smile on her face felt forced, as did the cheerful tone she adopted. She shouldered her rucksack, making it clear she intended to leave.

Marney frowned again, a flash of anger in her eyes. "You can't go yet. Tim and Pete want to take us to dinner." She emphasized the *us*, and Silver ducked her head in apology, avoiding the pressure she could read in her friend's disappointed gaze.

"I really need to go, I'm sorry." Her parents had raised her to always be polite and considerate, which was all well and good if everyone else was equally polite and considerate. When dealing with forceful personalities, it was her natural instinct to give in to their demands. It made her the perfect victim for those of a less altruistic nature. She was tired and bored, and if she didn't make a stand now, there would no doubt be an awkward, probably unpleasant, end to the evening when Pete made it clear he expected some form of reimbursement for dinner. Shuddering at the thought of wrestling with him in the backseat of a cab, Silver found just enough backbone to smile and scuttle away from the table.

"Hey! Hey, where you going?"

She quickened her step at the sound of Pete's voice behind her. Turning sideways, she wriggled between a large, boisterous group entering the bar and escaped the brush of fingers against her sleeve. Hurrying across the road, she eschewed her usual bus stop. Best to put a bit of distance between herself and the bar, just in case Pete decided to pursue her further.

She turned the corner, buttoning her coat against a sudden chill wind. The businesses lining the street were all closed. Their thick security shutters covered in graffiti and the piles of garbage clogging up the drainage channels in the road gave the street a seedy, rundown air. Lights shone at a few windows in the apartments above the stores. Muffled music and occasional shouts reached her ears. Arriving at the intersection, Silver paused, recalling the address she'd looked up earlier. Tina lived less than three blocks away. It wouldn't take more than a few minutes to check in on her. *Might as well try and get something positive out of this busted evening.*

A large, black truck swerved through the intersection, running a red light, and Silver stepped back sharply from the edge of the curb. A pounding beat poured from the open windows of the truck, and a crowd of youths jeered from it as it sped past her. Ignoring her building sense of trepidation, she hurried along the sidewalk in the same direction. Vehicles passed in both directions, no taxis though, she noted. Hopefully, there would be a bus stop near Tina's and she could catch one heading in the right direction.

Just my luck. The tricked-out black truck sat directly in front of Tina's building. The front end blocked the sidewalk, the driver having ridden up the curb and abandoned it. Silver skirted around it to mount the shabby, broken steps of the apartment block. Rusted railings covered the lower windows. Tiny balconies holding makeshift washing lines, a couple of sad-looking plant pots, and a motley array of belongings that had spilled out of the upper apartments lined the top two stories. None of the buzzers on the wall were labelled, but the front door to the block had been wedged open with a large brick.

Hesitating for a moment, Silver studied the hallway. The lighting was spotty, large stretches of darkness between the weak glow of a few overhead lights. Ignoring the queasy twist in her stomach, she checked the apartment numbers on the first couple of doors—103, 105, 104 opposite. Returning to the small entrance lobby, she ignored the elevator and opted for the staircase. The smell of stale garbage and urine increased the farther she climbed, making her glad to escape the confines of the stairwell into the third-floor corridor.

The lighting in the narrow hallway was even poorer than on the ground floor. Angry male voices spilled out from an open doorway halfway down, and Silver did a quick count of the doors. Her pulse rate increased when she realized the argument was coming from Tina's apartment. *This is a really bad idea.* Concern for her student warred with her belated sense of self-preservation. The shouting increased, accompanied by sounds of a struggle. Fear lent wings to her feet, and she fled for the stairwell, holding her breath against the unpleasant stench.

She stumbled from the building, one hand pressed to her chest over her racing heart. Looking up and down the street, she searched in vain for a bus stop or passing cab. The slap of running feet and shouts sent her spinning off to the left, and she huddled against the side of the building away from the group of men who poured down the steps in pursuit of a skinny kid, dressed in a thin, gray sweatshirt and jeans that hung low, revealing most of his backside. The low-slung pants impeded the boy's flight, or so it appeared when he staggered a few steps. The door to the apartment block banged closed. Silver flinched at the noise. Crouching low, she muffled a cry when the boy tripped and fell on his face.

"Stupid, dumb fuck! No one steals from me," a voice crowed from the top of the building steps, and a chorus of hoots, insults, and encouragement rose from the group of men arrayed around the steps.

Silver blinked at the boy on the ground, watching the dark stain spread across the back of his pale sweatshirt. Her brain refused to cooperate, shying away from the truth her eyes were telling her. A high wail escaped her lips, and she slammed a hand over her mouth, turning in horror toward the scarred face of the man at the top of the steps. *Click. Click.*

"Motherfuckinpieceofshit," the man snarled. Like a slow-action replay, his hand swung around to point a large, black gun at her head.

Run! Sweat pooled at the base of the spine as she stared death in the face, but her feet refused to obey her brain's frantic screaming instructions. Tires squealing, a battered truck barreled down the street.

"Shit! It's the fucking cops," one of the men shouted, and the rest of the group ran toward their abandoned truck.

The scarred man sauntered down the steps as though he had all the time in the world, his eyes fixed on Silver. "What the fuck are you looking at, bitch?"

She shrank farther back at the menace in his tone, unable to tear her gaze away.

"Come on, Razor, come on man. It's those fuckers from the task force," a voice yelled from the open door of the black truck. The battered vehicle bounced up the curb, trying to cut off their escape route.

"You're dead, bitch." The man sneered. A thick gob of spit landed on her cheek, and she choked on the sobs bursting from her throat. Cowering lower, she ignored the cold press of the dirty concrete beneath the thin pantyhose covering her legs. She tucked her head into her lap. Sobbing and shaking, she waited for the inevitable bullet to strike her down. *I'm going to die without ever having an orgasm.* The ridiculous thought sent a bubble of hysteria up her throat, and she curled her arms around her knees, laughing and crying at the same time.

A few moments later, a gentle, but insistent hand

shook her shoulder until Silver lifted her head. Concerned brown eyes, crinkled at the edges, studied her in concern. "Are you hurt, miss?"

Another bubble of laughter erupted from her. "So-sorry," she managed through the inappropriate giggles.

"It's all right, darlin'. You're in shock. Can you stand up and let me check you over?" He urged her to her feet, his voice calm and soothing. She let him twist and turn her, making sure there were no injuries. "She's fine, Charlie," he called over his shoulder toward a second man crouched next to the fallen boy.

"Same can't be said for this poor kid. Any idea what happened?" His partner scrubbed his face with one hand.

"Razor," Silver whispered, and the man holding her spun his head back toward her.

"What did you say?" His grip on her arm tightened, and she flinched. Easing his hold, he touched her cheek with his other hand, forcing her to look away from the body and up at him.

"Razor shot him. That's what one of the other's called him, I think. He was going to sh-shoot me, but then you arrived." Her body shook, the realization of how close she'd come to death striking home.

An engine rumbled in the near distance, and Charlie cursed loudly. "Those fuckers are back. Better get her out of here until we can get some support."

The man holding her arm was already in motion, leading Silver to the battered truck. He opened the door, shoved her into the back, and piled in after her. Charlie slid into the driver's seat, crunching gears.

"Step on it, Charlie."

His partner didn't need the instruction and was already racing down the street away from the black truck. The man beside her fastened a seat belt around her, patted her knee, and settled his body in the opposite corner of the rear seat. His position enabled him to keep an eye on both her and the road behind them.

He pulled out his phone and made a succession of rapid calls, the first one to his captain. He rattled off a stream of information that stunned her in the level of detail he'd accumulated in those few minutes on the street. Keeping his attention fixed on the rear window, he finished his conversation and dialed another number.

"Hey, Derek, it's Jesse. I have a situation, and I could do with some help." He paused for a moment then spoke again. "No, no, Alexa's fine. I need a place to hide someone for a few days, though."

Chapter Two

The phone on the rough-hewn wooden table buzzed like an angry wasp. Kirk Matheson spared it an evil look, but otherwise ignored it, completing another round of chin-ups on the iron bar screwed into the sturdy crossbeam holding up the roof of his remote cabin. A matching set of bars were drilled into the wall, like rungs on a ladder, and a medicine ball hung suspended from the beam a few feet away.

Sweat ran freely down his chest, soaking into the waistband of his loose-fitting pants. The interior of the building matched its owner—all hard edges and practicalities. It served a useful purpose but offered little in the way of comfort. When the pack relocated into the neat bungalows that formed the heart of Moonlight, their recently established home, he'd opted for the abandoned cabin standing in a tangled thicket of Myrtle oak trees about half a mile from town.

Town might be stretching it when describing Moonlight. More a crossroads people ended up at by accident rather than intent. They got enough passing traffic to support their small community enterprises—a diner, a gas station, a convenience store—but the pack remained protective of their privacy. The Internet provided an employment haven for them, too. The anonymity of the screen meant they didn't have to work face-to-face with clients, didn't have to endure the relentless nosiness of working in an office with humans.

Derek may have frowned at Kirk's deliberate choice to isolate himself from the pack, but the others breathed a sigh of relief. No one wanted a neighbor who reminded them of the dark deeds committed to ensure the remnants of their little pack survived.

To his relief, the irritating noise ceased, and Kirk switched from the bar to the thick, padded bench beneath the window. Lying on his back, he grabbed two massive dumbbells and commenced a rapid set of flys, working the muscles of his barrel chest. The twice-daily routine kept him busy, kept him focused on his mission. Kirk was a weapon, a blunt-force trauma to be wielded at his alpha's instruction. The phone buzzed again.

"Motherfucker," he snarled, dropping the weights with a thud onto the nonslip mat beneath the bench.

Only one person had his number, and Kirk had already pushed the limits of disrespect by ignoring the first call. Stripping off the leather-grip gloves on his hands, he grabbed the phone and thumbed the answer button on the simple handset. No fancy smartphone for him. He didn't need record or photo-capture capabilities, didn't need Internet access for research. He wasn't an investigator like the others who worked for Derek Sawyer as part of The

Defenders, the pack's private security agency.

"I'm sorry to interrupt, Kirk." The alpha's smooth, controlled tone betrayed no annoyance at his minor attempt at rebellion.

"Who is it this time?" *Straight to the point, no time for chitchat. Can't let that clever bastard start digging around in my head.* Derek saw too much with those sharp eyes of his. Being the biggest wolf didn't automatically make you an alpha. Something Kirk would be forever grateful for. Taller and broader in both human and animal form, he still lowered his eyes before the utter dominance Derek exuded. Let others lead. Let them deal with the living, breathing members of the pack. Kirk had enough trouble handling the ghosts.

"Female. Human. Meet us in the diner in fifteen and I'll explain more." The handset went dead next to his ear, so he dropped it back on the table. Tossing the towel over his shoulder, he headed for the shower. The bathroom in his cabin occupied a full third of the overall floorplan. The wall tiles were plain white, the floor tiles gray, and a square of mirror hung above the white sink unit to assist on those rare occasions he decided to shave the thick scruff of beard from his jaw. The shower, by contrast, was a study in luxury. The waterfall shower head complemented a selection of wall jets to pound the aches from his muscles. A wide bench ran the length of the rear wall.

He'd saved every penny he had to replace the crappy old bathroom, spending hours online studying until he could do the installation work himself, even fitting an underground heat pump to ensure he had piping hot water whenever he wanted. Not like he didn't have plenty of time on his hands these days. Killing and plumbing—hell of a fucking skill set.

Settling in Moonlight gave the surviving members of their pack a chance to breathe again. A chance to live in relative peace without the desperate gnaw of fear twisting their guts. They'd been on the run for too long following the destruction of their habitat by developers. Hunters with their bloodlust and rival alphas with a taste for power had thinned their ranks even more, driving them south to the wilds of Central Florida. The pack had begun to settle and rebuild, and Kirk had no place among them anymore. He knew this, had come to terms with it, even if Derek had yet to acknowledge the fact.

After shoving his sweat pants down over his legs, he tossed the soft material into the basket on top of several other pairs waiting for the wash. With a sigh of pleasure, he stepped into the shower stall and flicked on all the jets. Hot water blasted from every direction, tempting him to linger in the steamy cocoon, but he had less than ten minutes left to get to the diner where the pack held all their meetings. Reaching for the bottle of all-in-one shower gel, he scrubbed the sweat from his skin and shut off the water with a brief flicker of regret.

It took a matter of seconds to towel-dry his short hair and pat the water from his upper body. He wandered into the bedroom, a thick white towel wrapped around his hips. Chewing on his toothbrush, he surveyed the sparse contents of the large dark-wood armoire standing in the corner. The heavy piece matched the solid bedframe—antiques he'd found in an old secondhand store and restored to a perfect luster. YouTube had a fucking video for everything these days.

A couple of white button-down shirts and a few more black ones hung next to matching monochrome T-shirts and a handful of pairs of dark pants. Selecting a black shirt and faded black jeans, he pulled a pair of black trunks from one of the lower drawers and dressed quickly. A pair of well-worn sneakers completed his outfit. He snatched up the keys to his pickup then ran down the small flight of stairs leading from the cabin to the rough track connecting his home to town.

It would be almost quicker to run to the diner than drive, but he would need his transportation to assist with disposal. The bed of the truck already held his equipment—a thick tarp, rope, and bricks for weight. Reversing his vehicle into the switchback he'd hewn through the thick undergrowth, he ran a mental map of pre-selected locations through his mind. Myakka River State Park held myriad hidden spots, and the gators were always grateful for an easy meal. This wouldn't be the first female Kirk had dealt with for the pack, but it would be the first human female. *It's all the same to me.* The lie sounded convincing enough in his head, and he pushed any qualms he had deeper. The pack came first. Last. Always.

Bumping down the rutted path, he wove the truck through the thick sheets of Spanish moss hanging from the trees on either side. He didn't bother with lights, his wolf-enhanced eyesight cutting through the dark night with ease. He turned off the track, onto the main street through town, and parked outside the diner. A handful of vehicles stood in a haphazard row, including a battered truck he recognized as belonging to Jesse, one of the human detectives from the local sheriff's department who'd mated into the pack. It didn't make sense for him to be present. Although he'd accepted the man, and his partner Charlie, into the pack, Kirk made damn sure to keep his dirty pack secrets from them to avoid any conflict of interest.

Feeling uneasy, he approached the diner. The blinds were down, the closed sign hanging in the window. No light escaped from inside to alert passing traffic. He rapped his knuckles on the door, studying the dark road over his shoulder until he heard the lock unsnap and he could slip inside. Stopping just inside, he held the door at his back. Testing the air with his sensitive nose, he scanned the room. He filtered and dismissed the scents he recognized. Derek, of course. Rand, his second-in-command. The humans, Jesse and Charlie.

Fear, sweat, and a faint hint of blood all did their best to mask a sweet twist of honeysuckle. Kirk focused all his senses on the small figure cowering in the far corner of one of the booths. Nothing about the woman gave any indication of a threat, but it wasn't his job to question his alpha's decisions. He hadn't been summoned for a slice of pie and a cup of coffee. He marched across the room and grabbed the small female by the arm, dragging her from the red, padded bench seat and halfway toward the door.

"What the fuck, man?" Charlie shouted, rising from his seat around a central table.

Kirk ignored him, ignored the fragile bones of the slender wrist grasped in his thick hold. Jesse rounded the table, reaching out to grab Kirk. Lucky for him, his hand closed on empty air when Rand restrained him. Snarling, Kirk shoved the woman behind him, trapping her between the door and his broad body. He rounded on the four men, claws forming, teeth elongated and ready to snap. They'd summoned him for a reason, and there could be no room for doubts. The woman had been deemed a threat, and the situation would be handled.

His way.

Chest heaving like a set of bellows, he studied the four men arrayed before him. Charlie and Jesse looked furious, glowering and struggling against the hold Rand had on them. The pack second smirked, although Kirk didn't see anything to laugh about. And Derek looked thoughtful, studying him with those probing eyes of his.

"You're hurting me," a soft, feminine voice whispered into his back. What did he care about crushing her? She wouldn't feel anything soon enough. Still, he eased a few inches away and forced his minor shift back under control. The tips of his fingers tingled where his claws retracted, but another sensation—or rather the lack of one—distracted him. He missed the slight warmth once the woman was no longer squeezed tight between himself and the door.

"Calm down, Kirk." Derek didn't bother to raise his voice over the curses pouring from Charlie.

"Not me that needs to calm down. You summoned me, and we both know what that means. Not my problem you chose to involve those who have no business here." He sneered at the two human males and pressed against the plump little female until her ripe breasts nestled against his spine. Her small hands braced at his hips, and she made a futile effort to push him forward again.

A look of sadness flittered across the alpha's face,

and he shook his head. "You are what I made you, Kirk, and I am sorrier for that than you will ever know. I should have realized you would jump to conclusions as to why I called you."

A deep growl rumbled in Kirk's chest. He was proud to serve Derek and the pack. Every step he'd taken down the road to hell had been taken with the sure knowledge no one else in the pack would have to perform an evil deed for the greater good. He carried the sins of their survival so they didn't have to.

"I don't need pity. I just need your orders. I've got a dump site already picked out. She's only a little thing so the gators will make short work of the body."

"Body? What fucking body? I didn't bring her here for you to kill her, you fucking freak!" Jesse yelled, straining against Rand's hold.

Kirk ignored him, keeping his eyes fixed on Derek's face. He couldn't ignore the sobs, or the scent of terror, rising from the woman though. Her tears soaked into his shirt, her fingers scrabbled against his back where she fought to get free from his weight restraining her. An inexplicable urge to gather her into his arms and comfort her rose in his chest. He snarled again, using his anger to fight down the conflicting emotions.

"This is Silver Ellis, and she needs our protection. Needs *your* protection. My orders are for you to take her back to the cabin with you and keep her safe from harm," Derek said.

A bark of bitter laughter escaped Kirk. The alpha must have taken leave of his senses. "I don't do protection."

"You do now," Derek retorted. Nodding to Rand, he indicated to him to release the two detectives. The second wore a shit-eating grin a mile wide, and Kirk wanted nothing more than to choke the fucker. He opened and closed his fists, releasing the tension from his shaking fingers.

"You can't be serious about this, Derek. I came to you for help. You can't trust this bastard with my witness," Jesse sputtered.

A hard look settled on the alpha's face, and he turned the full force of his power on the human. "You are pack now, Jesse. Do not forget yourself again. I trust Kirk more than any other person in this room at the moment."

Jesse rammed his hands on his hips but lowered his eyes in submission. He blew out a breath, nodding once. "Okay, okay."

Derek dismissed him again, leaving it to Rand to lead a still protesting Charlie away and remind him about pack protocol. Folding his arms across his chest, he leaned back against the table behind him, body language relaxed. "Silver witnessed a murder tonight. The gang involved will stop at nothing to get their hands on her. Jesse asked for my help, and I agreed."

Kirk opened his mouth and closed it again with a quick snap. His mind reeled as he tried to process everything. Derek trusted him? The woman soaking his skin with her tears wasn't to be killed? He would have to share his home with her? See her curvy little body every day, hear her sweet voice, smell that delicate honeysuckle fragrance?

No fucking way!

The rational side of him rejected the whole scenario as preposterous. The animal side licked its lips at the thought of all that sweet, plump goodness stretched out on his bed. Blood rushed to his cock, swelling his flesh to the point of pain. He dropped his arm casually in front of him. Trying to shield his physical reaction, he sent a pleading look to his alpha.

Derek quirked an eyebrow at him. "Something you wanted to say, Kirk?"

Shit! Shit! Shit!

He swallowed around the protests in his throat and shook his head. "How long do you think I'll have to keep her?" *A week? A month? Forever?* Shaking off the ridiculous notion that any woman could belong to him, he tried to concentrate on the brief discussion between Jesse and Derek.

"It'll take some time to pull the investigation together. The evidence from the scene will need to be processed. The labs are slammed, so it takes a while for the test results to come in. We need to hit the streets. Tensions are running high after last night." Jesse paused and gave Kirk a hard look. "I'll come over tomorrow and take a proper statement from Silver."

"No. You won't. You don't come to my place. We'll meet you here, but not tomorrow." A protective surge flooded through him. "She's suffered a trauma." Silver was his responsibility now, and nothing would be allowed to upset her.

Turning his back on the other men, Kirk bent his knees to meet her red-rimmed eyes. Blotches marred the creamy skin of her cheeks. Tears still trickled from the corners of her eyes, although her sobs had quietened. Ignoring her flinch, he cupped her face, using his thumbs to wipe the wetness away.

"You're safe," he murmured, keeping his voice

low.

Fear and disbelief warred in her gaze, and he searched for something else reassuring to say. Women were soft, easily hurt, and he was too damn rough for all this touchy-feely shit.

"I'll kill anyone who tries to hurt you." There, that should do it.

"Kill?" Her voice shook, and the tears flowed harder over his thumbs.

He twisted his lips into a tooth-baring smile. Chicks liked smiles, didn't they? She wasn't anything like the kind of woman he spent time with. He studied her clothing. Her drab coat, the fussy blouse with a big bow tied at the neck, the shapeless skirt hanging below her knees.

His gaze traveled lower, and he growled at the sight of her torn stockings. Bloody scrapes showed through the ruined nylon, the source of the blood he'd scented when he first arrived. Dropping to his knees, he held her still with one hand on her hip while he used the other to brush away the dirt and stones embedded in her skin.

Turning his head, he glared at Charlie, the first person he spotted. "She's hurt, and you did nothing about it!"

Not waiting for a response, Kirk stood up, swinging Silver into his arms. Holding her weight easily with one arm, he yanked the diner door open. He cleared the distance between the building and his truck with one leap, bending his knees to absorb their landing without jostling her.

Big, brown eyes stared at him in shock, but she didn't resist when he lifted her into the passenger seat of the truck. He reached around to snag the seatbelt, smoothing her skirt over her knee when he saw it had rucked up her thighs. He tried the smile again, and she reared back in the seat. *Poor kitten must still be in shock.*

The four men lined the porch of the diner, expressions a mixture of confusion, anger, and humor. Kirk nodded once at Derek. "I'll text when she's ready to talk."

Jesse stepped forward, handing him a battered rucksack. "This is all she had with her. I need that statement."

"When she's fucking ready, and not a moment before, you hear me?" Kirk snarled. He climbed into the truck. Tossing the rucksack on the wide dash in front of the steering wheel, he slammed the door harder than intended.

"I hear you." Derek's quiet words drifted across the night.

Chapter Three

S ilver resisted the urge to shift in her seat. She didn't want to do anything to draw the attention of the man next to her. Her fight-or-flight mode had switched off somewhere along the journey in the back of the police truck, leaving her tired, scared, and confused. The brief ray of hope she'd experienced when Detective Farrell mentioned taking her to a safe place shattered the first time the big man beside her fixed his hard gaze on her. The memory of the look in his mahogany eyes as he calmly discussed places to dump her body sent a shudder of fear through her.

"What is it?" The man froze in the middle of starting the engine, head swiveling in all directions.

He leaned closer, wide shoulders brushing against the front of her body. She pressed farther back into her seat, trying to avoid the contact. He stared past her at the inky darkness. His weight pressed nearer, and she held her breath, not wanting to risk his anger. He turned his face. The thick beard covering his chin scraped along her jaw, his warm breath ghosted against her cheek. Nudging her head up and left, he buried his nose in the spot just beneath her ear and drew a deep breath.

"Something scared you, kitten. Tell me what."

She felt more than heard his low voice rumble through her. How could she answer him? Only a fool would tell a man who so casually talked of death that they were the source of terror. His clean, zesty scent confused her senses. A cold-blooded killer shouldn't smell like fresh citrus. He should smell of dark things, ugly things.

Something wet tickled her neck. *Oh my God, did he just lick me?* She needed to get him away from her. Straining, she tried to spot the diner from the corner of her eye. If the other men were still there, she might stand a chance. The darkness blinded her. The light that had spilled onto the front porch from the open diner door had gone. Nothing stirred outside. She was on her own.

"Nothing. I thought I heard something, but it was nothing. I'm tired that's all. It's been a strange night, and I could do with a hot drink. Is your cabin far from here?" The words spilled out from her quivering lips, ending in a brittle laugh.

He *snarled*. She couldn't think of another way to describe the harsh noise that ripped from his throat.

"Don't lie to me, kitten. I can smell it on you, even through the miasma of fear clinging to you. I'll ask you one last time, what are you afraid of?"

"You," she whispered.

One heartbeat. Two. Three. She held still, braced for his reaction. A rusty, strange sound vibrated along her skin, and it took her a moment to understand what it was. Laughter. He wheezed again, as though unused to making such a sound, and pulled back to his own seat. Relief flooded her system for a moment before cold realization struck.

They'd left her in the control of a madman.

The engine of the truck roared into life, and she jumped at the sudden harsh noise. Grinding the gears, the man gripped the steering wheel, guiding the truck along the main road. There were no streetlights in the little town, and she had no idea how he could see anything without headlights, but he maneuvered the vehicle as if they were in broad daylight. A sharp wrench of the wheel, and they were bouncing down a rutted track.

Silver stretched her hands forward to brace against the dashboard, but the truck hit a deep pothole, throwing her off balance. She grabbed instead for the handle hanging above her door, her right hand scrabbling for a hold on the seat beside her. Warm, calloused fingers grabbed hers, placing them on a rock-solid, denim-covered thigh. The truck lurched again, and she dug her fingers in. The muscle beneath them didn't give. A sliver of light broke through the tree line, the moon's soft rays picking out shadowy, twisted limbs.

Something trailed along the window beside her and she let out a shriek, cowering away from the glass as far as her seatbelt would allow. His fingers tightened over hers, making her aware he steered the truck one handed.

"It's just Spanish moss. Nothing will harm you while you are in my care."

Silver closed her eyes, trying to calm her racing heart. She wanted to believe him, but the claws of panic had sunk too deep in her brain. Pressing her head into the leather rest behind her, she focused on what she knew. *My name is Silver Ellis. I'm a teacher at Johnson Middle School. I'm an only child and I live at 243 Oak Street. My social security number is 342....*

"What are you doing?"

Her eyes flew open, and she realized they'd come to a stop. Soft yellow illuminated the cab from the overhead light. A warm breeze brushed against her from the open driver's door. The man. *Kirk.* That's what the others in the diner called him. Kirk stared at her, body half-twisted as though he'd paused in the middle of climbing out.

"I'm sorry?"

"What's with the name, rank, serial number routine?"

A blush heated her cheeks. "I didn't mean to say it out loud. It's a technique my father taught me when I was little, a way to center myself after having a nightmare. Focus on facts you know. A way to remind myself what is real."

His rusty laugh barked out again. "I hate to disappoint you, kitten. This is real life, and the boogeyman is your only hope."

He slid from the truck, the cab's interior light cutting out when he slammed the door closed behind him. Her eyes didn't get a chance to adjust to the sudden darkness. The light blinked on again as he opened her door, reaching across her to unfasten her belt. His cool citrus scent washed over her.

"Do you get them a lot?" His quiet question puzzled her for a moment.

"Nightmares?"

He nodded once, eyes fixed on the lock of her seatbelt. She studied his short, dark hair in the weak light. A few threads of silver glinted amid the jet-black strands. A thick, white scar bisected the beard on his jaw, running from beneath his chin to the middle of his cheek in a slash. She wondered what had caused such a devastating injury, then decided she didn't want to know.

"I used to. Full-on night terrors." The memories of too many nights sweating, thrashing, and screaming as she tried to escape the confines of her blankets threatened to rise. She pushed the monsters back into the darkest corners of her awareness. Kirk cocked his head, and the monsters swirled in the deep pools of his eyes. She swallowed and flicked her attention back to the scar on his jaw.

"They took me to the doctor in the end. He said they were normal, something I would grow out of. I did for a while, but then they came back." When her mother died, leaving a twelve-year-old girl to the tender, but unprepared care of an older father. He'd done his best, could not have loved her more if he tried, but there were just some skills he lacked.

Large arms banded around her back and beneath her knees, and she found herself lifted from the seat into Kirk's embrace again.

"I can walk," she muttered, the words masked beneath the sound of the door slamming when he shoved it with his elbow.

"The gravel needs renewing," he said.

His hearing must be as keen as his eyesight.

"You might twist an ankle by stepping in a pothole, even in *those*."

She followed his gaze to the low-heeled, lace-up shoes on her feet, her pride bristling at the disparaging tone. There was nothing wrong with her choice of footwear. She spent most of her day on her feet; why would she totter around in ridiculous heels?

She thought again about the magnificent boots Marney wore and sighed. Without a mother to steer her through her teenage years, Silver had never developed the confidence to embrace a style other than the plain, simple clothing her father preferred to see her in. That uniform of skirts and blouses had followed her into adulthood. The few times she'd tried something more suited to her age, she'd felt ridiculous and overdressed.

His heavy tread on the short staircase leading to a single-story building chased away her musings. Squinting in the faint moonlight, she tried to make out some features of the squat structure, but it was a hopeless effort. An overhanging roof cast the building in shadow. The darkness it created swallowed them as Kirk carried her beneath it onto a wide porch.

Shifting her weight in his arms, he half-slung Silver over his shoulder, one beefy hand gripping her ass. She squeaked in protest, but he ignored her, unlocking the door with his free hand. Expecting him to put her down, or at least return her to a less intrusive hold, she instead found herself carted through a dark room and into another smaller one. He dropped her onto some kind of shelf, keeping one hand on her waist. She rested her hands on a smooth, hard surface. Exploring further, her fingers came in contact with something colder. *A sink.*

A touch on her leg startled her, and she brushed it away. "Don't you have any lights in this place?"

The heat of his body moved away, and she raised a hand to shield her eyes from the white light when he flipped a switch on the wall. She blinked a couple of times, adjusting to the brightness. Her mouth fell open as she took in the bathroom. Like something out of a high-end hotel, or a luxury penthouse out of one of her favorite shows, the space glistened and gleamed. Polished tile covered the walls and floor, and a thread of pure lust struck her at the sight of the enormous shower taking up over half of the space.

"Oh, wow!" She gasped.

"You like it?" The shy pride in his voice—nothing like the gruffness she expected from him—drew her attention.

His focus remained on the glass stall, and she took the opportunity to study him for the first time. She didn't think she'd ever met a man so tall. He filled the room with those broad shoulders of his. Muscle and sinew roped his biceps and forearms, and a dusting of dark hair covered the golden skin. She knew the same muscles padded his chest from being nestled there. His torso narrowed a little into his hips, giving way to thick legs that stretched on forever. He cleared his throat, and she peeked up, heat rushing to her face at being caught looking.

"Stand up," he ordered.

Using her palms to balance herself, she lowered her feet to the floor. He moved closer, until she could feel the heat pouring off his body. He jerked her skirt up, hands fumbling at her waist. Shock froze her in place for a moment, and then she began to struggle.

"What...what the heck are you doing?" She tried in vain to shove his hands away, but she might as well try to push a brick wall. He stripped her pantyhose down her legs, crouching at her feet to unlace her shoes.

"I need to get the dirt out of the wounds on your

legs before you take a shower." He squeezed her calf, lifting her leg to remove her left shoe, repeating the action with her right.

Her hose disappeared, flung into a corner wastebasket, and Silver found herself perched back on the counter. Kirk nudged her legs to the side, removing the biggest first-aid kit she'd ever seen from the cupboard beneath the unit. She boggled at the contents. It looked like something a field medic would carry into battle.

"You're certainly well prepared," she said, watching him rifle through the kit with brisk efficiency.

He grunted, placing a bottle of antiseptic and a pair of tweezers beside her. "Lift your foot; rest it on my leg," he instructed, patting his thigh to show where he wanted her to place it.

The last of the adrenaline left her system, and a bone-deep weariness settled over her. Even moving her leg seemed like too much effort. Wrapping his callused palm around her calf, Kirk propped her foot in position and bent his dark head over it. The motion caused her skirt to ride up her thigh, but he gave no sign of noticing, dabbing at the bloody graze with a warm washcloth.

He cleaned around the wound, his actions surprisingly gentle for such a big, fierce man. Silver relaxed a little under his ministrations, watching him work. The cloth brushed over a painful spot, making her catch her breath.

"Sorry, kitten," he murmured, dropping the cloth into the sink beside her. He took up the tweezers, nudging at whatever was stuck in her leg.

"Ow!" Silver tried to tug her leg from his grasp,

but he held on until she quit moving.

"Grab onto my shoulder. It looks like a piece of glass. Be brave for me, okay?" He glanced up through his brows, a softer look in those deep, brown eyes than she'd seen before.

Catching her lip between her teeth, she curled a tentative hand over the cord of muscle close to his neck. The cold metal instrument dug into her flesh, and she squeezed her fingers, small nails digging into the solid mass of his shoulder. He pressed the tweezers deeper, making her whimper. A sharp tug and he held up the tiny piece of glass, displaying his prize with a look of satisfaction. Blood trickled from her leg, and he used the cloth to wipe it away.

"I think that's the last of it. No point in putting anything on it until after you've had a shower." He lifted her other leg, nodded once, and released it. "Nothing in there that won't wash away."

Dropping back on his heels, Kirk stared at her. "How the fuck did you end up in such a mess, kitten?" he asked, shaking his head.

I have no idea.

Feeling uncomfortable under his intense gaze, she raised a hand to rub the back of her neck. Her fingers caught in the tangled remains of her bun. Ripped knees, filthy coat, hair hanging half down her back. She must look a fright.

"Do you have a comb?"

He blinked once, shook his head, and pushed up to his full height. He rubbed a hand over his short hair. "I don't have much call for one, sorry."

"I had one in my rucksack." She looked around the room, as though her missing bag might be hiding in the corner.

"It's in the truck. Jesse gave it to me when we left the diner. Have your shower, and I'll go and fetch it for you."

She nodded in gratitude. After shrugging off her ruined coat, she began to unfasten the cuffs on her blouse. The pale material was stained, and she caught a whiff of sweat from her earlier fear. If his sense of smell was half as good as his other senses, then she was amazed he could stand to be in the same room as her. The shower beckoned like a Siren, but she hesitated. There wouldn't be any point getting clean if she had to put the same clothes back on.

"I don't have anything else to wear," she said, toying with the bedraggled-looking bow at the neck of her blouse.

Kirk paused in the bathroom doorway, studying her over his shoulder. His gaze traveled the length of her body, leaving her tingling from the ends of her fingers to the tips of her toes. The heat in his eyes unmistakable, he caught and held her gaze.

"I'll find you something to put on." He exited the room, pulling the door closed behind him.

She slumped back against the sink unit, hand fluttering at her throat, heart racing a mile a minute. No man had ever looked at her with such awareness. She'd had a date or two, even got as far as going to bed with a kind, if ineffectual, male friend at college. The experience had left her disappointed, embarrassed, and in no hurry to let another man put his hands on her body.

Kirk wouldn't fumble his way around, wouldn't pinch her skin with his nails, or spill his seed before she got close to an orgasm. A pulse throbbed between her legs as she pictured his big body pinning her underneath him. She shook herself. *Not half an hour ago he was discussing how to dispose of your dead body, and you're fantasizing about him?*

It had to be a reaction to the shock. Had to be.

Face flaming, she unfastened the limp bow and fiddled with the buttons on her blouse. The door flew open, the noise making her jump. Kirk glowered at her, all the earlier kindness wiped from his face by a vicious snarl.

He tossed her bag and a folded bundle of clothing at her feet. "Get in the fucking shower, Silver!"

The door slammed closed, the bang even louder than when he'd flung it open, if that were possible. The rush of lust she'd experienced vanished beneath a fresh wash of fear. Fingers shaking, she twisted the lock on the door and stripped off her clothes.

Hot water thundered down from the huge showerhead, blasting her from all sides via the jets fixed at various points on the walls. She closed her eyes, lifting her head to let the water cascade over her face. A sob rattled in her chest as she massaged a handful of shower gel into her hair. Steam rose, filling her senses with the fresh, clean scent of the man on the other side of the door. The tight knot in her chest unraveled, and Silver let go. Hot tears of fear and shock ran down her cheeks, disappearing into the drain in a swirl of citrus bubbles.

Chapter Four

Kirk paced the floor of the cabin, feet moving faster and faster as he tried not to picture what was happening behind the bathroom door. The water would be running down all that creamy, ripe flesh, driving the cold from her skin the way he longed to do with the heat of his body. The smell of her arousal hit him the moment he stepped out of his bedroom with her bag slung over his shoulder and a T-shirt and a pair of boxers for her to wear. The urge to claim her, to back her luscious body into the shower and fuck until they were both mindless rode him like a freight train.

"Fuck it!" He abandoned his pacing, jumping up to grab the chin bar. A harsh sound echoed from the other room, and he gripped the bar until his fingers turned white. She was crying, for fuck's sake.

He hauled himself up and down, locking his ankles so the full weight of his 300 plus pounds hung from his shoulders. Not his problem. He wasn't a nursemaid. He wasn't there to kiss her boo-boos and make everything better.

Kissing, shit! He shouldn't have thought about

kissing. His dick turned rock hard. He imagined trailing his lips down her neck to those delicious-looking tits. Would her nipples be pink or brown? Her hair was dark, but given the paleness of her skin, he'd have to look to know for sure.

Jumping away from the bar, he yanked the door open and ran out into the night. The flat soles of his running shoes sent gravel pinging against the side of the truck as he sprinted past and ducked into the trees. The bulge in his jeans made it awkward to run, but he pushed himself harder. He needed to put some distance between him and the human in his cabin before he did something stupid. A rough, scarred bastard like him was no good for a delicate little thing like Silver Ellis.

The difference in their sizes would make the logistics themselves a challenge. He'd have to kneel beside the bed to get their hips at the same height. Maybe lie on his back and haul her into his lap, have her ride him like a pony. More blood rushed to his cock, and he stumbled to a standstill.

Resting his hands on his hips, he blew out a breath, turning in a circle to get his bearings. He knew every inch of the lands surrounding not just his home, but the whole town. His flight had carried him farther than he'd realized—a good mile from the cabin.

Silver should be out of the shower right now, though it would take some time to dry her hair if it was anywhere near as long as he imagined it to be given the size of the knot pinned at her nape. The wet strands would flow down her back like melted chocolate, the ends brushing against the curve of her ass. And he'd left her alone, with the door wide open.

Derek had placed her in his safe-keeping, and yet here he was, hiding in the trees, thinking with his dick instead of his brain.

"Shit!" He ran flat out, retracing his steps, ducking branches and leaping over fallen logs without a single thought for his own safety. The pack relied upon him to do what must be done, and he would do it. Even if his balls turned blue in the process.

"Silver!" He charged through the open door of the cabin, claws out. The door to the bathroom swung open, and she stared at him, brown eyes wide. He hid his hands behind his back before she could see his twisted nails.

"What is it? What's the matter?" The T-shirt he'd left for her swallowed her frame, the hem skimming to mid-thigh, the edge of his boxers peeking out beneath it. She'd scooped the wet mass of her hair over one shoulder, and he could tell from the comb in her hand she'd been in the process of untangling it.

She looked sexy as all hell.

A wave of possessiveness gripped him at the sight of her wearing his clothes. Even though it was clean, the material would carry his scent, would leave a trace of him on her skin. He wanted more than a trace. He wanted to mark her so deeply, everyone would know who she belonged to. What the hell? She didn't belong to him; he needed to get a grip. Needed her to get a grip, wrap her little hand around the thick shaft pressing against his fly.

"Argh!" Kirk slammed the front door closed, putting all his frustration into it. Something cracked, and he scowled up at a split in the frame. Turning his glare on Silver, he tried to get his mind back in the game.

"Are you hungry?" he demanded.

"What?" She blinked at him, a look of utter confusion on her face.

"Are. You. Hungry. It's not exactly a difficult fucking question." He marched into the kitchenette area of the open plan space, anything to avoid the hurt glistening in her eyes. *She better not start crying again.*

He yanked open a cupboard and pulled out a couple of large cans of tomato soup. It was getting late, and he didn't have the patience to cook a full meal. Silver would be better with something easy to eat, given everything she'd been through. A lance of something suspiciously like guilt stabbed into him. He banged a pan onto the small stove, dumped the contents of the cans, and turned the heat on beneath it.

A small sniff behind him sent tension arrowing up his spine, but he refused to turn around, reaching instead for a thick loaf of bread and a sharp knife. She sniffed again.

"For the love of God," he snarled, spinning on his heel, brandishing the knife in front of him.

She screamed.

Dropping the comb, she fled for the bathroom. He lowered his head in despair, scowling when he saw the seven-inch blade of the butcher knife he'd grabbed. Clenching his fingers around the handle, he turned his attention to the bread, hacking off a few lumps that in no way resembled slices. He retrieved a tub of butter from the refrigerator, slapped some on the bread.

Gloop.

"Goddamnit!" he cursed, sucking the splash of hot soup from the back of his hand.

He grabbed a spoon to stir the bubbling pot, scraping the liquid from the bottom before it had a chance to stick. The door to the bathroom inched open, but he kept his back to it. He followed Silver's cautious progress across the room with just his ears, noting the soft scrape when she bent to retrieve her comb from the floor.

"Soup's ready. Grab a seat," he said, shaking his head in frustration at the small squeak she emitted at the sound of his voice.

"I'm not hungry," she whispered, and he heard her edging toward the bathroom.

"Sit your fucking ass at the table, Silver. Right this minute." Hauling his temper under control, he snatched a couple of bowls and plates from the overhead cabinet.

He filled the bowls, slung the bread on the plates, and strode to the wooden table. She perched on the very edge of one of the chairs, the one closest to the bathroom door. He blew out a breath, dumping everything down. Returning to the kitchen, he filled two tall glasses with milk and placed them with care in the neutral space between them. Taking the seat opposite her, he avoided her eyes and reached for his spoon.

"Shit!" Shoving his chair back so hard it skidded about five feet, he marched to the drawer where he stored the silverware then retraced his steps to the table, spoons in hand.

"Eat." He brandished one of them at her, but she made no move to take it. He clattered the spoon into her bowl, causing the soup to slosh over the side onto the tabletop. Stomping to his seat with a growl, Kirk shoved the hot liquid into his mouth in a series of rapid movements. The bowl was half empty by the time he paused to grab a chunk of bread. Silver's meal remained untouched before her.

"If you don't eat, I'll feed you myself," he snapped.

Her head jerked up. *Easy, man. Take it easy, she's tired and scared.* Forcing down his natural aggression, he gave her a reassuring grin. She recoiled, dropping her gaze to her lap. He wished to hell she'd stop flinching every time he tried to be nice. Women were weird.

Kirk reminded himself once again why he lived alone. Happily, peacefully alone.

"You need to keep your strength up. I promised Derek I would look after you, and he'll be pissed at me if he thinks I didn't do a good job taking care of you."

A snort of derision flew from her nose, and she clamped her hand over her face. The sour fear smell returned, tainting the intoxicating mix of honeysuckle and citrus he'd been trying hard not to notice. He scrubbed a hand over his head. Just as well he kept his hair short, or this bloody female would have him pulling it out by the roots.

"You're safe here. I'll protect you." He moderated his tone, pitching his voice as low and quiet as he could.

"That's great, but who'll protect me from you?" she muttered.

Christ! He kept his head down, mopping the rest of his soup up with the remainder of his bread. Pushing away from the table, he gave her some space, making a big performance of washing out his bowl and the pan.

The faint chink of silverware on china filled him with relief, and he continued to clean the kitchen, wiping the cloth over the surfaces, the front of the refrigerator, and the top of the stove. He kept himself busy, pretending not to be aware of every single move she made.

He tracked her movements as she approached, holding still when she placed her dishes in the sink next to him. He waited for her to retreat, heard the frame on his old armchair creak as she settled herself into it. The chair stood next to the window, the farthest point she could get from him and still be in the room. He rinsed her bowl and spoon, took the time to dry them, and put everything away in the cupboards before he turned to look at her.

She sat cross-legged in the middle of the chair, head down so her long hair hung forward, the ends touching the floor. Gripping close to the roots, she pulled the comb through, in long even strokes. The rhythmic motion mesmerized him, and he tucked his fingers into the front pockets of his jeans. They itched to take the comb from her, to stroke away the fear and tension he could see in her stiff shoulders.

Tearing his eyes away, he frowned at the near-full glass of milk she'd left on the table. Seizing the excuse to approach her, he picked up the drink and carried it over. He carefully placed the glass on an orange crate that served as a side table then forced himself to move away. He sat opposite her on the unfamiliar couch. The cushions were firm beneath his ass, harder than the chair. The couch was reserved for visitors, not that he ever invited anyone over. The only pack member who came to his cabin was Derek, and he rarely stayed long enough to bother sitting down.

Shifting his weight until he could find a comfortable position, he watched and waited. Silver continued to comb her hair, teasing the last few knots loose. Gathering the thick strands between her hands, she twisted it round into a tight ball, using a band around her wrist to secure it in place. She lifted her head, cheeks flushed from leaning down for so long. He held back a sigh of disappointment. He wanted to see it free, framing her face and flowing down her back. His mind conjured images of it spread across the white pillows on his bed, and had to cross his legs to hide the return of his infernal erection. Damn, he would end up with a permanent imprint of his zipper on his cock if he kept thinking about her like that.

"Drink your milk."

"I'm not that keen on milk. Do you have any coffee?"

He shook his head. He didn't do stimulants of any sort, wouldn't risk anything that might elevate his temper. They didn't last in his system for long. His enhanced shifter metabolism burned everything fast—calories, caffeine, alcohol. Still, he didn't like feeling off balance for even a moment. Not when it could cost someone their life.

Another reason he needed to get Silver out of his life as soon as possible. She upset his equilibrium, fucked with his head more than drugs or booze ever could. He studied her again. What was it about the little human that stirred him up? There was nothing remarkable about her looks, pretty enough, but not the kind of woman to turn heads. She didn't flaunt herself. Given her dowdy clothes and lack of makeup and adornments, it appeared she did the opposite.

That hair, though.

Kirk longed to run his fingers through it, to wrap it around his fist until he controlled her head. He wanted to pull it until she creamed all over her thighs while he fed his cock into the hot cavern of her mouth.

"What are you doing?"

He blinked and shook his head, his reverie disrupted by her question. "Huh? Nothing? Never mind." A strange tingle heated his neck. *Jesus, now I'm blushing?* Thank fuck his beard would cover the worst of his reaction.

"You make strange noises, sometimes. Growling, snarling. Like a dog." She fiddled with the comb, twisting and turning it over in her hands. Her jaw-cracking yawn saved him from trying to explain the animalistic responses she brought out in him, and he pushed to his feet.

"It's been a rough day; I'll show you where the bedroom is."

He moved around the room, turning on the bedside lamp, sending a soft glow across the white linen. The sheets were fresh enough. He'd only slept in them once, and he always had a shower after his evening round of exercise. He dug out a set of sweat pants from the top drawer of his dresser and glanced toward the doorway. Silver hovered on the threshold, teeth worrying her bottom lip. Ignoring the urge to pull her to him and soothe the tiny injury with his tongue, he frowned at her.

"Is there a problem?"

She looked at her feet, the bed, him for a brief second, and then back to the floor. "There's just the one bed?" Color flooded her pale cheeks.

He tucked the sweat pants under his arm, grabbed one the pillows from the bed, and brushed her out of the way as he left the room. "Don't worry, kitten, your innocence will remain intact. I'm sleeping out here."

Tossing the pillow onto the couch, he popped the top button of his fly. He couldn't wait to get out of his damn jeans. His cock seemed determined to remain at half-mast, and the constricting material had gone beyond uncomfortable. She didn't move from the spot by the door.

Staring into her eyes, Kirk unfastened the second button. The rosy heat in her face went from pink to flame red. She lifted her hands to her burning cheeks but made no move to leave.

He took a step forward, hand on the next button. "Stop looking at me like that. You don't want this, kitten," he muttered, trying to convince himself as much as her.

"Don't want what?" The telltale wavering in her voice proved his point.

"A man like me in your bed. Be warned, Silver, there is a fraction of decency left in me, and you are straining it to the limit. I'm giving you a chance because you've had a bad time of it. If you don't get out of my sight in the next three seconds, I'll have you on your back with my cock so deep in your pussy you won't be able to walk for a week. Lucky for you, I don't do virgins." Empty space greeted his final words.

Kirk studied the closed bedroom door, wrestling

his wolf instincts back under control. The animal wanted out. The wood would prove no barrier. One kick and he could be balls deep in all that honeysuckle goodness. He jammed his hands on his hips and drew in a deep breath, held it for a count of five, and released it on a sigh. Whatever the wolf wanted, the man was right. Silver didn't want a man like him, more beast than anything else.

He rapped his knuckles on the door. "There's a spare toothbrush under the bathroom sink. I'm going for a run, so you'll have the place to yourself for a while. I won't go far, and I'll lock up behind me."

Silence greeted him.

He padded out of the cabin, locking the door as promised. No one would come around, but she didn't know that. He tucked the key in a notch he'd cut beneath the third step and shucked his jeans. Calling the wolf, he welcomed the rush of strength as fur rippled down his spine. He launched himself forward, landing on four wide paws. Little chunks of gravel rattled beneath him as he bent his head and forced the wolf to run. Given half a chance the damn thing would crash straight back through one of the windows.

Muzzle to the ground, Kirk completed a full circuit of the land around his home, testing scents, checking markers he'd left remained undisturbed. Satisfied no intruders had dared to encroach on his territory, he ran. One word pounded in his head as his paws struck the ground in a rapid tattoo. Mate. Mate. Mate.

Chapter Five

Thick tentacles wrapped around her throat, dragging her deeper into the inky-black water. She thrashed, clawing at the slick flesh, trying to gain purchase on the alien creature. Her nails scratched the warm, hairy surface, desperate to loosen the suffocating mass, fighting to draw oxygen even though she knew the fetid water would fill her lungs. She couldn't breathe, couldn't think as the monster turned her, tugged her into its protective embrace.

Your name is Silver Ellis. You're a teacher at Johnson Middle School. You're an only child and you live at 243 Oak Street. Your social security number is....

Her eyes flew open, a hoarse rattle burning the back of her throat.

Black. Everything was black.

She tried to move, couldn't. The lingering threads of the nightmare sucked her back under. She couldn't breathe, couldn't think as the monster squeezed her tighter in the depths of hell.

"Silver? Come on, kitten, wake up for me. Jesus

Christ, wake the fuck up."

The blackness resolved into two dark circles framed by thick lashes. Heat surrounded her, and a warm, golden glow filled the room. *Kirk, the cabin.* Reality chased the last vestiges of the nightmare away, and she could breathe again.

"I'm okay." The wobble in her voice said otherwise. She took another, steadier breath and tried again. "I'm okay, thank you."

The deep furrow between his dark brows eased a fraction, and the solid weight of his body shifted to the side. A heavy leg still trapped hers beneath it, and her shoulder remained burrowed into his side. She should be scared being close to someone so dangerous, not feel such relief at his looming presence. Tension melted from her bones, and she relaxed her fingers that clung to his forearm in a death grip. His soft grunt drew her eyes, and she gasped in horror at the bloody scratches marring his tanned skin.

"It's nothing," he snapped when she tried to protest.

"But—"

"Nothing."

With a nod, she swallowed the apology on her lips. If he wanted to play the tough guy, she didn't have the energy to argue with him about it. Trying to lift her head, she stopped, wincing at the sharp pain in her scalp. The thick plait of her hair, woven before she went to sleep, lay trapped beneath the arm he'd wrapped around her shoulders. A noise rumbled in his chest, vibrating down her side. She froze.

The look of worry on his face morphed to something else, and a predator studied her from behind those deep-mahogany eyes. Her heart fluttered, not entirely in fright.

"I can't move," she murmured.

He held her gaze, unblinking. A stain of embarrassment flushed her throat and cheeks. She'd always been quick to blush, but her reactions to this man were ridiculous. His thick lashes shuttered down, back up, and the hungry look was gone. The solid reassurance of his body lifted away, and she followed his progress from the room with her eyes.

A thick, white towel covered his hips, doing nothing to disguise the evidence of his erection. Everything about him was big. *Everything.* She swallowed hard, tugging the covers up to her nose, hiding the fresh bloom of color heating her face. He didn't stop, didn't look back at the bed, swinging the door shut behind him.

She strained her ears, heard the springs of the couch squeak in protest as he settled himself on it. Gripping the edge of the sheet, she waited. And waited. Sleep tugged at the corner of her awareness, but she brushed it away.

A deep rumble rose and fell, rose and fell. Kirk's snores soothed and disappointed her at the same time. Turning her face into the pillow, imagining it still held a trace of his warmth, she let her eyes drift close.

They danced around each other for the next couple of days, an unspoken, coordinated effort to avoid anything approximating intimate contact. Kirk refused her offers of help, telling her off the moment she stirred from the big armchair. He bitched about her presence, bemoaning her invasion of his space, her disruption of his routine. He'd storm out, saying he needed a bit of peace and quiet, returning a few minutes later claiming to have forgotten some urgent task.

She kept her nose buried in one book or another. The choice of reading material was limited—technical plumbing guides, and what appeared to be every piece of literature ever issued by the Florida State Parks Department. She didn't know what he did for a living; he would only say that he worked for Derek. The relationship between the two men seemed more than employer-employee, but he hadn't responded to her attempts at digging.

Whatever his job entailed, he needed to be fit for it. Her favorite two hours of the day were his workout sessions. Watching the sweat roll across his thickly muscled body sent her heart racing and her thoughts spiraling. The steamy scenes in the romance novels she devoured in the quiet confines of her apartment had been abstract. The images they drew were unlike anything in her limited experience. Seeing Kirk strain his body to the limits provided flesh to those remembered stories. Hot, sculpted flesh she longed to trace with the tip of her tongue.

The tension between them reached the boiling point, and Silver feared her face would be permanently red from the dreams that replaced her nightmares. Dreams of his weight pressing her deep into the mattress, strong legs spreading hers wide. That huge cock of his surging between her thighs. If she didn't get some relief soon, she would scream.

Or spontaneously combust.

Needing to escape the suffocating atmosphere in the cabin, she glanced up from the plumbing manual sprawled across her lap. He moved around the kitchen in that silent way of his—always surprising in a man of his stature. Her offer to tidy up after breakfast had been met with an order to "park your fucking ass." Closing the heavy book with a thud, she gathered her nerve.

"I'm ready to talk to Jesse."

His head snapped around, and she wrestled against the urge to squirm beneath his scowl.

"You need to rest."

"I'm fine. Bored, but otherwise fine. I need to speak to him while the information is still fresh." She glanced at her lap then back up. "A boy died, Kirk. I can't let that go just because I'm scared."

A mutinous look crossed his face, but he didn't refute her words.

Time stretched between them.

"Fine." With a shake of his head, Kirk turned back to his task, slamming a few cupboard doors in the process.

That went better than I expected.

She waited a couple more minutes then raised her other issue. "I'll need something to wear. I can't go to the meeting in your underwear."

Something snapped, and he turned back to her with a handle from one of the cupboards clenched in his fist. *Oops.*

She'd learned over the previous forty-eight hours that his bark was much worse than his bite. He yelled. A lot. Stomped around, bossed her about, and generally annoyed the hell out of her, but there was no malice in it. His dire warnings about being a bad person, mutterings of evil deeds he'd committed, no longer scared her. When he threatened to turn her over his knee and spank her, she'd experienced such a rush of desire it left her light-headed.

He tossed the handle into the sink and stormed into the bedroom, returning in a clean pair of jeans and a white T-shirt. He paused beside her chair.

"Do you have a suitcase at home?"

"Yes. There's one on top of the wardrobe." She pictured him moving around her private spaces. "I can come with you. It'll be quicker, besides I know where everything is."

He cut her off with a raised hand. "You stay here. Take a nap. I want you rested before you make your statement tonight."

Orders issued, he snatched up his keys and left, securing the door behind him. The truck roared to life, wheels crunching on the driveway. Quiet descended. She waited five minutes to be sure he wouldn't return then set to work.

Take a nap, my ass.

Two enforced days of sitting around had given her more than enough time to study the cabin. He kept it neat, but there was an air of neglect about the place. It performed a function, providing shelter from the elements, but there was nothing about it that said *home*.

Folding the waistband of her borrowed boxer shorts over to prevent them from falling down, Silver ran through the mental list of chores she'd made earlier. She hit the kitchen first, checking cupboards and drawers, locating cleaning products, which she set out on the table. Rolling up her metaphorical sleeves, she got to work.

***

Going to Silver's apartment had been a

monumental mistake. He knew it the second he closed the door behind him and her honeysuckle scent surrounded him. It filled the entire space, teasing his senses, layering his skin until he felt like she was wrapped around him.

The main living space had a cozy feel about it. Mismatched antiques rubbed shoulders with overstuffed furniture covered in cushions. The warmth of her personality echoed from every surface, photographs, knickknacks—a peaceful life full of smiles.

Books littered the place, spilled out from bookcases lining one wall. A large television squatted on an old chest in the corner. The floral-patterned sofa was angled to face the set and he settled into it, knowing at once that this was Silver's spot. Her pretty natural fragrance lingered in the crocheted blanket folded over the back of the three-seater. An open paperback lay facedown on the side table. A basket of wool, needles, and a pattern book rested beside his foot.

He could picture her there, feet tucked underneath her, blanket over her lap as she watched a film, or read. He smiled at the cover of the book. *How to Tame a Rake* sounded more interesting than one of his plumbing manuals. His fingers traced the soft material and he tugged it down, folding the blanket into a neat square. It got chilly some nights in the cabin and although it didn't bother him, thanks to his wolf metabolism, she would be more susceptible. He set the folded blanket to one side and placed the book on top of it, using a scrap of paper to mark the page. A few other books were stacked on the table, so he added them as well.

Forcing himself to move from the comfortable sofa, he explored the rest of the small apartment. The array of bottles in the bathroom confused the hell out of him. *Why did women need so much crap?* He grabbed a toiletry bag he found beneath the sink and swept an armful of products into it, not bothering to check the labels. Dropping the bag on the pile forming on the sofa, he headed for the bedroom.

A bedspread scattered with bright red poppies covered the queen-sized bed. Another mountain of cushions rested against the pillows, and he made a mental note to add some to the items he'd gathered on the sofa. Silver would feel more relaxed if she had a few familiar possessions around the cabin.

Refusing to examine his motives for wanting her to be comfortable in his home, he yanked open the wardrobe and shook his head. Rows of skirts, blouses, sweaters, and long-sleeved dresses greeted him. No T-shirts, no jeans, nothing practical for living in the middle of the woods. He lowered his gaze to the neat pairs of sensible shoes. No running shoes, either. He tugged a few random items out and tossed them on the bed.

Her suitcase sat on the top of the wardrobe where she'd said. He threw the clothes, books, blanket, and cushions inside. He started to close the case, remembered her request for underwear, and pulled open the drawer of her bedside cabinet. His mouth dried at the sight of lace-edged scraps of silk in delicate pastel hues.

With trembling hands, he lifted up a pair of sky-blue silk panties. They were some type of shorts, and his cock filled to bursting at the thought of them cupping the rounded curves of Silver's ass. A matching bra lay folded neatly beneath. Scooping up two handfuls of sheer delight, he shoved them into the case and closed the lid.

Carrying out one last sweep of the place, he noticed the corner of a wooden box peeking out from beneath the bed. He crouched down, pulled it out, and flipped the lid. Photographs, cards, letters. He nudged through the contents, a strange burning sensation in his chest. He closed the box with a snap and tucked it under his arm.

Stowing the suitcase and box in the passenger side of the truck, Kirk checked the street for signs of anything suspicious. Satisfied his visit had not been noted by anyone, he pulled away from the curb, heading for the Walmart Supercenter off I-75.

The wolf snarled in his head at being surrounded by so many humans, and he was inclined to agree. Harsh smells assaulting his sensitive nose, he stood just inside the entrance, studying the large hanging signs until he located the department he wanted. Shouldering through a pair of gossiping mothers, he cut down one aisle, angling left until he hit the womenswear section.

He'd checked the sizes in Silver's clothes before packing them, but the sight before him proved he'd underestimated his task. Racks of jeans, pants, tops, and sweaters greeted him. *Where the fuck I am supposed to start?*

Knowing he was out of his depth, he pulled out his phone and thumbed the single contact in his address book. It rang twice.

"Everything, okay?" his alpha asked.

"Fine. Silver wants to give her statement tonight."

"I'll set it up. Jesse and Charlie will be relieved." Derek paused. "Was there something else?"

"I need to talk to your mate," Kirk muttered.

"Riesa? What the hell do you need to speak to her for? I can hear people, Kirk, where are you?"

"Please, Derek." A hint of desperation entered his voice. He'd never begged for anything in his life. This was what bloody women did to a man. The other end of the phone went muffled for a moment then a soft voice spoke.

"Hi, Kirk. How can I help you?" The alpha's mate was a quiet woman, intuitive and insightful. She also carried a psychic gift that had helped to save the life of Rand's mate, Hannah, from a deranged scientist.

"I, umm, I need to pick up some jeans and stuff for Silver, but there are too many damn options. Who knew denim came in so many different shades? What's wrong with blue and black? What the fuck is the difference between boot-cut and low-rise?" He kept his voice low, shielding the mouthpiece with his hand as he whispered into it.

Her tinkle of laughter was swiftly covered by a cough. "Well, it depends on her body shape and size. Is she tall or short? Slim or curvy?"

He pictured the swell of Silver's hips, the plump cheeks of her ass just begging for him to sink his teeth into them and mark her.

Shifting against the pressure in his pants, he replied, "Small, a little shorter than you, and curvy. Yeah, definitely curvy."

Following Riesa's patient instructions, Kirk filled his arms with boot-cut jeans, yoga pants, and a selection of casual tops. With a couple of pairs of running shoes and some sturdy boots balanced on top of the stack, he paid and fled the store. Gulping in a few lungfuls of fresh air, he thanked the alpha's mate and ended the call with a promise to take Silver over for dinner.

Dinner. What the hell was he thinking? He and Silver weren't a couple. Would never be a couple. He wasn't cut out for a relationship, carried too many scars, too many deaths on his conscience to sully an innocent like her with the baggage of his past. Just as well they were seeing Jesse tonight. He could get a timescale from him. Once he knew an end date to their time together, he'd be able to get himself under control.

Chapter Six

Stretching her back out with a sigh, Silver dropped the dirty cloth into the bucket and grinned at the sparkling windows. Just increasing the amount of light coming in worked wonders for the place. The few pieces of furniture had been polished to a shine and the bathroom scrubbed until gleaming. It still looked too bare for her liking, no sign of personality. *There must be something.*

She swallowed a tiny frisson of guilt and searched through the drawers of the large bureau occupying one corner of the room. Suppressing the urge to read the handful of documents she found, she rooted around the rest of the contents. The few boxes contained practical items, spare parts, and random lengths of metal piping. No photographs, table linens, or hand-me-downs. Nothing to show the man who lived there had a past at all.

Sitting back on her heels, she tried to put everything back where she'd found it. It hurt her heart to wonder what had happened to Kirk to make him want to isolate himself. Her own memories were stored in a hope chest her father carved for her sixth birthday. Cards, pictures, and cheap treasures they'd picked up on vacations. It had been too painful for a while to look at them after his passing, but now she found comfort in their familiarity. She wished she'd asked Kirk to bring it back with him from her apartment.

Feeling tired and grimy after her efforts, she headed for the shower. However muddled her feelings about Kirk might be, her love for his shower would stand the test of time. Dumping her sweaty shorts and T-shirt on the floor, she climbed into the huge glass stall with a sigh of pleasure. The waterfall of hot water spilling over her head was her favorite thing. Wait, maybe it was the wall jets.

Untying the bun at the nape of her neck, she massaged her aching scalp. She loved having long hair, but sometimes the weight of it made her wish for a cute pixie cut. After pouring a large handful of the citrus shower gel into the mass, she worked the fresh-scented liquid from root to tip. Men had it so easy. One bottle for everything, not like the clutter of concoctions littering the shelves in her bathroom.

Fragrant steam filled the stall, coating the glass screen. The sharp aroma conjured images of Kirk in her mind, the ridges of his abs rippling as he performed endless knee-lifts while hanging from one of the wall bars. A bead of moisture trailed down the tiled wall, just like the beads of sweat trickling down his chest.

Turning in the shower, she caught her nipple in a blast from one of the wall jets. The nub of flesh peaked, and she shivered at the erotic brush of it against her sensitive skin. Feeling naughty, she held first one breast, then the other into the pounding stream. The tingling arrowed down her middle, lower still to pool between her thighs.

She twisted around, standing on tiptoe to try and aim another jet at the juncture of her legs, but it was too high. The one beneath, too low. Frustration mounting, she slid a hand down, rubbing her fingers over her clit. The slickness she found embarrassed her, excited her more. Reaching lower, she probed at her opening, staggering when she lost her balance on the wet floor. She caught her weight on the bench running along the back wall and sat down.

Lifting her legs, she lowered herself onto the wide shelf. A jet from the side wall spilled onto her knees. Scooting closer, she braced her feet on either side of the jet and opened her thighs. The hot water hit her pussy, sending shots of pleasure through her.

"God, oh God," she whispered, trying to absorb the sudden assault on her most private place.

It felt good, *so good*. She palmed her breasts, closing her eyes as she teased her nipples. There was too much sensation, making it impossible to focus on all the different sources at once. She stopped trying to rationalize it and just felt everything.

The image of Kirk rose behind her closed lids, and she pretended the heat pounding against her pussy was his tongue, his hands, his cock. Tighter and tighter, the tension wound within her until she feared something would snap.

Maybe there is something wrong with me?

She could sense her orgasm just beyond her reach, but no matter how she strained, she couldn't grasp it. Wriggling her hips in frustration, she shifted around until the jet hit just the right spot and her spine bowed, lifting her hips from the hard bench as stars burst behind her closed lids. Too much, it was too much to bear. She closed her legs, rolling off the bench to kneel beneath the cascade of the main showerhead. Crouching low, she shuddered and shook through the aftermath.

Wow!

It took a couple of minutes until she could get her legs back underneath her, her knees wobbling like a newborn foal. She rinsed and turned off the water. Her skin felt too sensitive to rub, so she wrapped a large towel around her body, a smaller one around her soaking hair.

Blaming the flush in her cheeks on the heat of the shower, she carried her dirty clothes and the contents from the bathroom hamper into the main room and loaded the washing machine. The familiar sound of gravel spattering outside caught her attention, and she stood on tiptoe to peer out of the high window next to the front door.

Kirk lifted her suitcase and, to her surprise, a bundle of shopping bags from a big-brand store. He unlocked the door, dropping the bags at his feet when he saw her next to the table.

"I told you to take a nap," he snapped. His frowning gaze swept the room before settling on her again. "What have you been up to?"

"I just wanted to show my appreciation for your hospitality." The way he scowled at her made her start to think it hadn't been such a good idea. He cocked his head, drawing a deep breath into his nose.

"You cooked a meal?"

She nodded. "Stew and some homemade dumplings. Nothing fancy." She loved to cook, and it had been too long since she'd had a chance to make a meal to share with someone.

The expression on his face softened. "Thank you." His nostrils flared again and he fixed his hot, dark eyes on her. A low sound rumbled deep in his chest. "Your face is red."

He stalked closer, and she stepped to the left, keeping the table between them.

Her hand fluttered against her cheek. "I took a shower. I think the thermostat was set too high."

His eyes fixed on the top of the towel where she'd tucked the loose end between her breasts. The thick cotton covered her more than the T-shirt and shorts she'd been wearing, but she felt naked beneath his close attention. He moved again.

She backed away, seeking the relative safety of the bedroom, but he changed direction and pushed open the bathroom door. Steam billowed out. The rumble in his chest increased to a full growl.

"What have you been up to, kitten?" His tone shifted from annoyed to a soft, silky purr. She shuddered. His voice stroked along her skin, like a thousand tiny fireflies flashing through her awareness. There was no way he could know what she'd been doing in the shower. He glanced at her over his shoulder, the heat in his expression sending pulses of pleasure straight to her core. *He knows.*

The material of the towel abraded her stiffening nipples. She licked her lower lip. She should be embarrassed, but the thought of those hot eyes fixed on her body while she touched herself sent her desire spiraling higher. Tugging the end of the towel free, she held it in her shaking fist for a long moment.

"Don't," he groaned, more plea than command.

"Why not?" Her lack of experience made her

nervous. Maybe she was misreading the signals, and he was trying to prevent her making a fool of herself. A man like Kirk would have women queuing around the block for his attention.

What would he want with me?

The excitement faded, and she tucked the loose end back in. "Never mind. I don't know what I was thinking."

She hurried toward the pile of bags beside the table. Hefting her suitcase, she retreated to the bedroom. A band of heat curled around her upper arm, his sure grip stopping her on the threshold.

"What were you thinking about, Silver?" he murmured.

Heart racing, she kept her head turned away.

"You," she whispered. "I was thinking about you."

He'd clung to his determination all the way home, but the sight of her wrapped in nothing more than a towel blew his damn mind. A myriad of scents greeted him. Cleaning products, a spicy stew, the shower gel he favored, all mingled in with that honeysuckle sweetness—his new addiction. He sniffed again, locking his knees to prevent from dropping to the floor when a musky tang hit. Arousal. The little human fidgeted from foot to foot, all rosy-cheeked and smelling of pleasure.

And according to her whispered declaration, she'd been playing with herself and thinking about him. The wolf surged forward, eager to taste, to rut and claim the delicate offering before them. The man had run out of patience also. Time to teach her a lesson. To show Silver exactly what kind of man he was. He could slake his need for her and make damn sure she never let him near her again. The more he thought about it, the more perfect the idea seemed.

He tightened his grip on her arm. "I'm going to fuck you, Silver." His declaration sent a shudder through her body. "Last chance to stop me, kitten."

Her spine stiffened, but she didn't move. Didn't look at him, didn't try to pull away either. He slid his hand down her arm, took the suitcase from her, and placed it on the floor. With a firm hand on her shoulder, he steered her into the bedroom, kicking the door closed behind him.

"Take off the towel, Silver," he ordered, spinning her to face him. She reached up, hesitated, and he snapped his fingers beneath her nose. Her eyes jerked up to meet his.

"When we're in here, you do what I tell you, when I tell you. This isn't hearts and flowers and happy-ever-after. This is fucking. I'll make it good for you, kitten. Make it so good, you'll be screaming my name, but we need to be clear right from the start."

Cheeks flaming red, she loosened the bath towel and let it drop to the floor. He sucked in a breath.

She was fucking perfect.

Her creamy skin undulated in all the right places. Rose-pink nipples, wide and begging for his mouth, tipped her ripe breasts. Her waist curved in above a generous pair of hips. Her frame might be small, but she would take everything he had to give her.

Thick, dark curls concealed her pussy, and he frowned, wishing he had the patience to cart her into the bathroom and shave her clean. *Next time.* Only there wasn't going to be a next time, he reminded himself. He closed the distance between them. Tugging the towel from her head, he caught the thick, damp strands of her hair in his fist as it tumbled free. Dragging her head back to the perfect position, he claimed her mouth. His teeth nipped her bottom lip hard. Taking advantage of her gasp, he shoved his tongue between her open lips and ravished the wet heat. His other hand fixed on her ass, lifting her to straddle the thigh shoved between her legs as he fucked her mouth over and over.

Damn, she tasted good.

He thrust again, licking the roof of her mouth, behind her teeth, tangling his tongue with hers. Little pants and moans echoed in her throat. The slight sting of her nails where she clutched his forearms for balance added an extra layer of pleasure.

Needing more, he ripped his mouth free, grabbed her hips, and tossed her backward onto the bed. She sprawled across the white cotton, chest heaving, legs open, giving him a glimpse of her glistening pussy. He ripped his T-shirt over his head, popped his fly, and shoved the denim and his boxers down in one movement. She gasped at the sight of his cock springing free, and he gave her a fierce grin.

"See what you do to me? My cock's been aching for you since the moment I saw you."

He toed off his shoes, kicking his legs free until he stood naked before her. Gripping his shaft, he stroked his dick, palming the sensitive head. Her eyes grew round as saucers, and she nibbled her bottom lip.

"Spread your legs, Silver. Spread them wide and hold yourself open for me. I want to see that pretty pussy of yours." She hesitated, and he growled. "Do you know what happens if you disobey me?"

The whites of her eyes flashed. *Good, she needs to be afraid of me.* "If you don't do what I tell you, I'll turn you over and spank your ass until it glows. And then...." He moved forward until his knees hit the end of the bed, looming over her. "And then, I'll spread that tight little hole and fuck you till you scream."

Her mouth dropped open, shock written large across her sweet face.

"Spread your legs, kitten. Last chance."

A part of him longed for her to resist, but she raised herself on shaky elbows. Using her hands to part her labia, she gave him a clear view of her pussy. Arousal shone, coating her lower lips and trickling down between the cheeks of her ass. Her mind might shy from the idea of him fucking her ass, but her body betrayed her excitement. *Shit, she's going to kill me.*

He crawled onto the bed, grabbed her knees, and forced her legs wider still, making room for his broad shoulders. "You smell so good, kitten. I can't wait to taste all that honey dripping from you."

She shuddered, but kept her hands in place. He lifted a finger, ran it the length of her pussy, and shoved it deep into her passage. Jesus, she was so fucking tight he would have a hell of job getting her to take his cock. He shuttled his finger in and out, added a second the moment the ring of muscles began to relax. The force of his hand lifted her hips, making her breasts jiggle and the air fly from her lungs on a gasping breath.

"Am I too rough for you? It's who I am, baby. Can you take what I need to give you?" He grunted, shifting one hand beneath her ass to lift her closer to his invading fingers.

"I can take it." She moaned. "Everything, Kirk, give me everything." Cream spilled from her entrance, coating his hand, dampening the sheets beneath them.

He pulled free, and she whimpered. Taking her hands, he lifted them from her pussy to her breasts, pressing her fingers hard around the burgeoning nipples. He tweaked the ripe points, twisting and tugging, showing her how he wanted her to do it.

"Pinch them hard, Silver. Pinch them to the edge of pain, and then a little harder still."

She followed his instructions, her head thrashing against the covers as she tweaked and tormented herself. *So fucking hot.*

Letting a rumble of pleasure build in his chest, he lowered his head and used his tongue to lash the tortured ends of her nipples peeking through her fingertips. She cried out, a shudder running through her body. Her hips twisted, rubbing her wet core against his rigid cock. He lifted his head to stare at her flushed face, meeting her gaze.

"Tell me what you need, baby." She lifted her hips, but he shook his head. "Not good enough. I'm half-crazed with the need for you. Make it clear you're ready for me."

"I want you inside me," she whispered, her voice hoarse.

"Where, baby? In your mouth, in your pussy, in your ass?" He would claim every part of her eventually, but let her think she had a choice.

She closed her eyes, took a breath, and opened them again. The look she gave him drew his balls up tight against his body. "Fuck my pussy, Kirk. I want your cock as deep inside my pussy as it will go. Take me, fuck me, own me."

Squeezing the base of his dick, he hoped he wouldn't blow his load the second he entered her wet heat. Those blunt words, combined with the pretty blush on her face, frayed the edge of his control. *She's human.* "Don't move." He jumped from the bed and ran to the kitchen, rummaging through the shopping bags until he found the box of condoms he'd thrown into the basket on impulse.

After hurrying back to the bedroom, he resumed his position between her thighs. Taking care not to rip the thin latex, he opened the packet then rolled the membrane over his shaft. He stroked his cock the length of her sex a couple of times, coating the head in her slick juices. Lining up against her entrance, he caught her gaze and held it as he pressed forward into her resisting flesh.

Using one hand to brace his weight over her, he fed his cock inch by inch into the boiling heat of her core, pausing now and then to let her body adjust to his girth. Her body clamped down around him, and she whimpered. Fighting the urge to ram home, he held still. He liked his sex hard and furious, but there was nothing appealing about the look of discomfort on her face.

Easing back, he froze when she dug her nails into his ass.

"No, wait," she muttered through gritted teeth.

Sweat dripped from his brow to land between her breasts. He forced himself to hold still, stroking his hands up and down her thighs where they clamped around his hips. "Relax, kitten."

She nodded once, biting her lower lip in that way he found completely adorable. Her legs loosened beneath his gentle caresses. She dropped them to the bed, parting her thighs to give him access to her clit. He licked his thumb and reached between their bodies, applying pressure to the sensitive nub. A gasp escaped her lips, one of pleasure this time, and he crooned soft words of encouragement.

"That's my girl. Take your time, kitten. Find what you need. I'll wait, Silver." He groaned, muscles shaking at the effort to prove his words. "But fuck, baby. Find it soon."

She shifted beneath him, and his cock slipped another couple of inches into the velvet fist of her pussy. He rubbed her clit while she rocked herself onto his shaft. Blood bloomed in his mouth from where he bit the inside of his cheek, but he let her control the moment until *finally* he was fully seated inside her.

His grand plan to scare her with his brutal side imploded the second she smiled up at him. The sweet trust gleaming in her chocolate-brown eyes stabbed deep into the withered remnants of his heart.

He was sold.

Silver Ellis is mine now.

Chapter Seven

The sensation of being sundered in two faded, replaced by a fullness unlike anything she had ever experienced. It was as though Kirk had found every hollow, empty place inside her and filled it with his essence. He surrounded her, possessed her to the point she couldn't tell where her body ended and his began.

This.

This is what she'd been made for, what she'd waited her short, uninteresting life for. Perhaps each soul was allotted a finite amount of pleasure, so her first quarter century had been uneventful to make up for this moment of completeness.

The look of intense concentration on his face held her captive. A bead of sweat trickled down his temple, and she brushed it away, sliding her fingers back to cup his head. His thumb nudged against her clit, bowing her body. His strength surprised her when he slid his other hand behind her back, lifting her easily to fuse their mouths together. His hold moved lower to cup her ass, shifting her weight until she straddled him as he rested back on his heels.

She opened her lips, greeting his kiss with a sigh of welcome. His tongue probed the depths of her mouth, and he lifted her hips before letting her drop, sinking his cock to the hilt once again.

"Mine," he growled into her mouth, the vibration of his chest rubbing her nipples.

Yes, yes. She was his.

Fucking he'd said, just fucking. But it didn't feel like that. It felt like hearts and flowers. Like happy-ever-after. All those things he swore he didn't have to give her shone in his gaze.

"Mine," he said again, voice fierce. Something stirred deep inside his mahogany eyes. He pressed his hips forward, pulling her body down to meet him. She tried to catch the rhythm, faltered, and he snarled. Rising up, he rocked her backward, spilling her onto her back, his huge frame pining her to the mattress.

"Mine." He thrust hard, driving the breath from her lungs.

"Mine." He palmed her knees, hooked her legs over his shoulders, and thrust again.

Over and over he pounded into her body, the slap of their flesh punctuated with that same word growled at the end of every thrust. She couldn't think, couldn't breathe as pressure built at the point connecting their bodies. She lifted her hands to clutch his shoulders, and he snatched them down, locking his hands around her wrists, holding her immobile.

She wanted to struggle, to free her arms so she could pull him closer, hold him to her while he destroyed everything she thought she understood about being a woman. The pace of his stokes increased, a look of desperation drawing his brows together.

"Take it, Silver. Take it all." He groaned, adding a twist of his hips that caught her clit in exactly the right way.

Her entire awareness narrowed down to that single point then radiated back out through every nerve in her body as her orgasm broke like a wave against a levee wall. She was the high tide and Kirk the strong embankment, buffering her passion, absorbing and controlling the force of it. He threw back his head and roared, hips shuddering as he poured his seed into the thin latex separating them.

She fell back on the bed, replete. He released the grip on her wrists, and her fingers tingled as the blood rushed back. The weight of his body vanished, and she mourned it for the few seconds it took him to dispose of the condom in the corner trash basket. His cock jutted forward, flushed with blood, throbbing.

"I can't," she whispered, watching him roll on a fresh condom.

"You can, kitten. You must. I have to have you again." Kirk flipped her onto her front, lifted her hips, and drove into her aching pussy. She lowered her face to the bedspread, surrendering her body to his demands.

The hard smack of his body against her ass echoed around the space, the scents of their sweat and desire mingling into a heavy musk. She closed her eyes, surprised when the ache between her legs blossomed into something else, something hungry lurking in the hidden reaches of her mind.

"Kirk," she moaned, lifting her ass higher to meet his downward thrust. He draped over her back, banding one hand around her shoulders, the other around her hips. His fingers probed, found, and pinched her clit, sending stars bursting behind her eyelids. She threw back her head, baring her neck, and his teeth sank into her vulnerable flesh as he came with her.

She must have lost consciousness for a moment. The next thing she knew heat brushed against her pussy, and she tried to bat it away, too sensitive to bear it.

"Shh, kitten. Let me clean you up and then you can sleep." Kirk knelt between her legs, bathing her core and upper thighs with a warm facecloth.

He dropped it on the floor beside the bed, gathering her close to his chest as he settled behind her on the bed. His lips settled on her shoulder, kissing the tender spot where he'd bitten her. Darkness pulled at her, and she let it take her, knowing the man who held her close would keep the monsters at bay.

**

She tried without success to peer around Kirk's broad body as they waited for the diner door to open. He held her trapped between the building and the street, head in constant motion so he could watch both the road and the diner. The town was deserted. The door creaked open, and he grabbed her around the waist, hauling her into the room. The four men she'd met—was it really three nights ago?—sat around the same table in the center of the room.

Inching away from his hold, Silver brushed nervously at the front of her new outfit. The long-sleeved, diamante-studded T-shirt hung loose over the first pair of jeans she'd ever owned. They clung to her hips tighter than she was comfortable with, but the gleam in Kirk's eye when she'd tried them on in their bedroom showed his appreciation of the figure-hugging denim. Little crystals sparkled on the back pockets, and she'd teamed them with a pair of pink slip-on running shoes. He'd been tight-lipped about the reason for his shopping expedition. He'd snarled about the impracticality of her wardrobe choices without admitting he'd chosen his purchases with care.

Jesse, the dark-haired detective, stood up, an encouraging smile on his face. He held out his hand toward her, and Silver would have moved closer if not for the restraining hold Kirk placed on her arm. He angled his body, placing himself between her and the men. The other two, Derek and the blond man whose name she couldn't remember, slid from their seats and moved to the counter at the rear of the room.

Some of the tension in Kirk's body melted away, and he inclined his head to them as he led her to the table. The other detective, Charlie, shook his shaggy hair away from his eyes and bent at the waist to lift a large tape recorder onto the table. He took his seat, fiddling with the machine, checking it was working while Kirk and Jesse held some kind of staring contest.

The detective lowered his eyes with a sigh, lifted them again to fix on Silver. "You sure you're okay to do this?"

"Yes." She swallowed. "Yes, I want to help in any way I can."

"That's great, Silver. We'll do everything we can

to keep you out of it, but your statement should be enough for us to obtain a warrant. Take a seat."

She glanced up at Kirk, waiting as per his tight-lipped instructions on the way over. He pulled out a chair and held it for her while she settled into it. Dragging another close, he sat beside her, curling his arm around the top of her seat. Jesse raised an eyebrow but didn't say anything as he spun his own chair so he could lean his elbows on the backrest.

"Why don't you start by telling us how you ended up in that part of the neighborhood."

Feeling self-conscious at all the attention, Silver took a deep breath and recounted everything she could remember, starting with going for drinks with Marney. Kirk snarled and muttered when she described her unexpected date, subsiding into a stiff silence when she placed her arm on his thick thigh. His hand clamped down on top of hers, stroking the back of her fingers. She pushed on with her account, explaining her concern for her absent pupil, the convenient excuse to escape the unwanted attentions of a drunken date.

The ugly scents of the dark corridor rose in her memory as she recalled edging toward the raised voices spilling from her pupil's apartment. Her heart raced, reliving the terror of those moments huddled against the wall. The metallic clicking of the gun. The fury etched on the scarred face of her would-be killer.

Bands of heat drove the sudden cold from her limbs, and she found herself perched in Kirk's lap, her cheek pressed against his solid chest.

"Enough!" he snarled, turning his back to the table. He cupped her chin, lifting her head to meet his eyes. The familiar scowl twisted his features, but she could see beyond it now. Could see the care and concern glittering in his gaze. "You don't have to do this. I won't let anyone live who is a threat to you, Silver. You're mine now, my mate to protect."

A chorus of groans and soft cursing from the men in the room met his violent declaration, but she ignored them, keeping her focus on Kirk.

"You can't go around killing people because they might cause me harm. That's not how it works."

"It does now, Silver." He dropped his lips to brush along hers. "There's some stuff I need to explain to you...."

"Kirk." Derek's sharp tone cut through the room, silencing everyone. Kirk lowered his head, curling around her until she felt smothered.

"She's mine, Derek. I claimed her."

"Claimed me?" Silver squirmed in his lap. "I'm not a prize in the lucky-dip of life. You don't get to *claim me.*"

She pushed against his arms until his hold slackened an inch or two. Twisting, she forced him to release her or risk causing her injury. She shot to her feet, rounding on him, hands on hips.

"One hot fuck doesn't give you the right to pull this caveman shit, buster!"

A bark of laughter escaped the blond man at the bar. "Christ, man. Three days in your company and she's gone from mild-mannered schoolteacher to owning your sorry ass!" He grinned at Silver, holding his hands up in mock surrender when she frowned at him.

"Not helping, Rand," Kirk snapped, drawing her attention back to him. He reached for her, tugging her firmly back into his lap. "Silver, please. Calm down, kitten."

"Calm down?" All the fear dredged up from the memory of that awful night morphed into anger. She balled her fists, pummeling the unyielding wall of his chest. He didn't flinch, not a flicker to show he felt any effect from her assault. Her hands stung. So did her pride, and hot tears prickled the back of her eyes.

"Fuck this," he grunted. Hefting her into his arms, Kirk slung her over one shoulder. Shock froze her in place. "You got what you need for now?" Not waiting for a response to his question, he carried her from the building.

His shoulder dug into her middle, making it hard to catch her breath. The steps of the diner thumped beneath his feet, rattling her teeth as he ran down them. Blood pounded in her head, and she opened her mouth to protest when he swung her off his shoulder, setting her with a bump on the front seat of his truck. He followed her in, crowding her body until she sprawled on her back, the full weight of his upper torso pressed into hers.

"Kirk," she gasped.

"Shut up, Silver. Shut the fuck up." He fisted her hair, shoving his tongue between her lips in a bruising kiss.

She knew she should struggle, not that anything less than a stick of dynamite would knock him loose if he didn't choose to move. The feel of his tongue thrusting in her mouth, the press of his cock against her pussy, short-circuited the synapses in her brain. She moaned at the hot pleasure pooling in her core. She sucked his tongue, drawing it deeper, holding it between her lips the way she longed to hold his cock in her aching center.

He ripped his mouth free with a snarl. "Damn, you make me crazy. I should put you over my knee and teach you a lesson."

Trying to ignore the moisture gathering between her legs, she shoved at his shoulders. "Teach *me* a lesson? Try teaching yourself some manners first!"

They glowered at each other. Chests heaving, they struggled for breath, struggled for control. Frustration, lust, fear. She watched the emotions flicker across his face, mirroring her own.

She couldn't tell which of them moved first, but their mouths fused again in a searing kiss. Whatever differences they had, this was one thing they agreed upon.

Need.

He pulled back, hands busy at her waistband. She reached for her top, had it halfway over her head before her sense of reason kicked in.

"Kirk, wait," she said, voice muffled by the cotton material covering her face.

"Can't wait. Need you so fucking bad, kitten," he moaned.

He leaned forward, dipping his tongue into her belly button as he worked the denim over her hips. Her eyes rolled back in her head, and there was a split second when she wanted to say "to hell with it" and just let him take her there in the parking lot. The notion of being caught wound her excitement higher. His tongue slipped lower still, probing the very top of her sex.

"What if someone sees?" she whispered, trailing off into a whimper of pleasure when the tip of his tongue grazed her clit.

As though on cue, the door to the diner opened.

Kirk reared back, shoving her legs into the truck, slamming the door shut so fast she barely had time to follow his movements. Rounding the hood, he jumped into the seat beside her, started the engine, and roared away from the lot. She would have tumbled to the floor, had he not braced her with one hand. Righting herself, Silver started to straighten her clothing.

"Get naked, baby. The moment I stop this damn truck, I'm gonna be balls deep in that hot little pussy." The raw lust in his voice sent liquid gushing between her thighs. She reversed her actions, stripping down to her underwear. He swerved, swore, and turned his eyes back onto the rough road leading to the cabin.

"Leave the bra," he ground out.

She wriggled free of her peach-colored silk panties, leaving the matching bra in place. Kirk had missed the drawer with her everyday underwear when he'd fetched her clothes, bringing instead the contents of her secret stash of impractical but sensuous lingerie.

The leather of the bench seat lay cool beneath her naked ass, another new sensation to add to her rapidly growing collection. She liked the contrast against her skin, leather and lace. The vehicle lurched to a halt, and he slid along the bench toward her, clawing at the button fly of his jeans.

"Get over here," he demanded, shoving his jeans and boxers halfway down his thighs.

She half-turned, contemplating the logistics in the confined space, but he had no patience. Grabbing her hips, he dragged her over his lap until she straddled him but with her back to him.

"Lift your hips," he ordered, stroking between her thighs when she did so. "Fuck, kitten. I love how wet you get for me. Lean forward, brace your weight on the dash."

She followed his instructions, shifting around until she straddled his broad thighs.

"Take your time, Silver," he said, guiding her over his shaft. The thick head of his cock breached her entrance, forcing moans from both of them. He felt even larger from this angle. *Is that even possible?*

"Good, good, good," she chanted. Pressing down, she relished the burn as his shaft stretched her open. His hands closed on her hips, a bruising grip that drove her higher. Using her leverage against the dash, she rocked back and forth, taking him deeper and deeper inside her body.

"That's it, baby. Take it, take it all. You feel so good, so fucking hot. You're burning me alive." He shifted his hold to her breasts, dragging the cups to the side so he could pinch her nipples.

Surging up to meet her down stroke, he twisted the hard peaks between his fingers, sending a blast of hot pleasure-pain rocketing through her. She cried out, clamping down on his cock as she started to come. He thrust faster, hips moving at a punishing speed as she quaked and shuddered around him.

"Goddamnit!" he yelled.

Hard hands gripped her hips, forcing her off his cock. *What did I do wrong?* Before she could ask, he yanked her hair, throwing the long length of it over the front of her shoulder. Hot liquid splashed against her naked back, his semen coating her skin. He curled his hand around her waist, pulling her back against his chest, heedless of the sticky mess smearing across his clothes.

"You make me crazy, Silver. It scares me how much I wanted to stay inside you, fill you with my seed—my child."

She dropped her head back onto his shoulder, unable to speak, shocked by how much she wanted it, too.

Three days they'd spent together, and already she couldn't imagine her future without him.

You're in big trouble, Silver.

Chapter Eight

He waited until her breathing slowed. Waited a few minutes more to be sure she was sound asleep. He'd taken her again, in the shower, in their bed. *Their bed.* She belonged with him now. In his mind, everything he had was hers now, too—theirs. Including his heart. She muttered something. He held her closer, smoothing his hands over the long waves of her hair draped over her shoulder. She settled again, and he risked easing away. Taking care not to disturb her, he slid his arm from beneath her body, tucked his pillow at her back, and rolled from the bed.

The wolf itched beneath his skin, desperate to get out. Being in the room with four other dominant males, even if two of them were human, had stretched his patience to the limit. Combined with the scent of his mate's fear, the wolf had wanted to rip and claw at everything and everyone around them. Channeling his aggression into sex had worked for a while, but the wolf would not be sated.

It wanted blood.

Gliding from the room, he padded on naked feet

to the front door. He considered locking it, changed his mind. The lock was linked to thick floor and ceiling bolts, the noise of them sliding into place would disturb her. He would stick close to the property. Nothing would be able to get within a few hundred feet of his land without him knowing about it.

He dropped to his haunches, summoning the wolf, letting the raw power of his beast flow through his veins. Leaves and gravel crunched beneath his paws and he took off, giving the wolf his head.

He ran.

Relishing the feel of the wind stirring his fur, the silence preceding him as creatures fell quiet the moment they sensed the predator among them. Crisscrossing the entire length of his property, he ran until his sides heaved. His path took him close to the edge of the clearing surrounding the cabin.

He considered calling it a night; Silver was waiting for him all warm and curvy. The thought of sliding in bed behind her, lifting her leg, and slipping his cock in her pussy pulled a deep growl from his throat. Movement distracted him, and the scent of a cottontail drifted on the soft breeze.

A flash of white fur betrayed the rabbit's path into the undergrowth. His wolf's hunting instinct kicked in. He launched himself forward, attention focused on the terrified creature. A little snack would take the edge off, settle the wolf further. He broke right, angling his path to cut the rabbit off. An extra burst of speed and the glorious taste of life filled his mouth. He flicked his head, snapping the rabbit's neck, silencing its desperate squeals. He settled on his haunches to eat.

His meal was over in a few mouthfuls. Belly full, muscles aching with exertion, he padded back toward the cabin. Blood coated his muzzle, filling his senses as he shifted forms in the shadow of the cabin. A thump came from inside, and his head snapped up. Light shone from the bathroom window. *Shit!* Shaking off the lingering traces of his shift, Kirk crept up the steps and into the cabin. He headed for the kitchen, rinsing the taste of raw meat from his mouth under the tap.

The bathroom door opened, and he turned, glass in hand. A soft glow from the light illuminated her beautiful hourglass shape, and his cock stirred in response. Thirsty after his run, he drained the glass of water and placed it on the counter. He closed the short distance between them, pausing when he noticed the flush on her cheek and the rapid beat of her heart. Fear and confusion twisted through the layers of honeysuckle and sex.

"What is it, kitten? What has you so spooked?" He cupped her chin, lifting her face until she met his eyes. She glanced away, making him growl, and her eyes flicked back to meet his. Her pupils were dilated, and not in response to his touch. He stroked her cheek with his thumb.

"I, umm...I had a bad dream. I woke up and you weren't there. I guess I panicked for a minute." Her tongue peeked out, and she licked her lower lip.

Distracted by the wet glisten of her mouth and eager to drive the fear from her eyes, he bent his knees to brush his lips over hers. She stiffened, tried to pull away, but he followed her retreat, pressing her back to the wall. His hands shifted, drawn to the silky mass of her hair. He loved everything about it, the texture, the color, the length. He stroked his way down the soft strands to the ends where they rested at the base of her back.

The tension melted from her limbs, and he captured her sigh of surrender in his open mouth. He deepened their kiss, thrusting his tongue between her lips, tasting, claiming. Her arms came around him, tracing the oblique muscles down his sides. Her touch fluttered against his skin like butterfly kisses, and her scent bloomed from fear to arousal.

He kissed her mouth, trailed his lips across her cheek to the stubborn jut of her jaw, lower to the delicate skin of her throat. She turned her head, giving him better access. The act of trust and submission left him gut shot, even if she didn't understand just how vulnerable it made her. Dropping to his knees, he cupped her breasts, pressing them together to bring her nipples to his mouth. He sucked the left one, using his teeth to draw it to a sharp peak, teasing the other with the rough pads of his fingers.

"It's you, it's really you." She sighed, dropping her hands to stroke his head.

He paused, glancing up her body. "Who else would it be, baby? That dream freaked you out, huh?"

She bit her lip then nodded.

"I've got just the cure for that." He moved lower, kissing every inch of sweet flesh, lingering on the gentle swell of her belly. She giggled, trying to squirm away, and he nipped her with his teeth. "I think this might be my favorite spot on your body."

"Stop it, silly." A delicate blush heated her throat.

"I'm serious, Silver. I love your softness." He nuzzled the indent at the top of her thigh.

"Fatness," she whispered.

He sat back on his knees, shocked. "What the hell? Don't talk about yourself like that, kitten. I love everything about you."

He cupped her ankles, stroked his hands up the back of her calves to her thighs. She shivered, the defeated look easing in her eyes. *Slow, slow, show her how you feel.* He'd been so caught up in his need for her, reveling in her eager responses to the pleasure he wanted to share with her. Wolves were sensuous creatures; touch was everything to them. Words were secondary, often unnecessary, and Kirk was less refined than most of them.

"You are the most beautiful thing I have ever seen." He coaxed her thighs wider, slid between them until his chin rested on the top of her pubic bone. Moisture glistening in her eyes, she stared down at him. A shimmering drop hovered on the rim, fell, and he darted his tongue out, catching the tear. He tasted the salt, wanted more, wanted to sip and savor every fluid from her body.

Gripping her thigh, he lifted her leg over his shoulder, opening her pussy wide to him. He ran his tongue the length of her sex, moaning at the taste of her. He pressed closer, thrusting deep into her channel, gathering more of her cream. Her nails dug into his scalp, urging him on, and he let go. Let the wildness in him rise and claim his mate.

She wobbled above him, and he used his hand to hold her up, not willing to be distracted from his feast. He ate at her, mouth roaming everywhere, sucking her clit, probing her entrance, even tracing lower to lick the puckered entrance to her ass.

"Kirk, you can't," she whimpered.

He turned his head, sinking his teeth into the soft meat of her thigh. "I can do anything I want, baby. You're mine now."

She shivered, but didn't protest again. He took her clit between his lips, sucking hard to distract her. Sliding a finger deep inside her pussy, he coated it in her cream. The muscle in her thigh twitched against his cheek, and he knew she was close. Increasing the suction on her sensitive bundle of nerves, he drove her to the brink then grazed the edge of his teeth over her clit.

Her name flew from his lips, and she grabbed at his head, rocking her pussy into his face. He teased his wet finger against the tight hole of her anus, pressing the tip just inside. She cried out, bucking her hips, soaking the lower half of his face with her juices.

"No more, no more," she whispered.

His hand against her belly held her in place. He pressed a final kiss against her clit and lifted his mouth, letting her slide down into his lap. She curled into him, snuggling like the kitten he called her. Lifting her easily, he carried her into the bedroom. They could both do with a shower, but she was already asleep.

***

"I'm not sure I can do this." Bright red stained her cheeks, and he suppressed a grin. He turned his face into her stomach to hide his expression.

"I want you to, baby. Please?"

Rain spattered against the window, and she shifted her legs under his head. "You promise not to laugh?" He nodded, and she began to speak in a soft voice.

He crossed his bare feet where they rested against the end of the sofa and settled his head in her lap. If the pack could see him now, they'd never believe it. The two of them had slipped into an easy domestic routine over the past week, doing the few chores they had together. Evenings were spent researching his latest project online while she worked on her crochet, or read one of the books he'd included with her things. The little smile playing on her lips piqued his curiosity, and with some gentle cajoling he'd persuaded her to read to him.

He knew it wasn't real, knew something would happen to shatter their peaceful bubble. But until the second it did, he was determined to make the most of it. Live in their little corner of make-believe where he was a decent guy, and she wasn't hiding from a criminal gang.

"The brush of his teeth against the pale, delicate skin of her neck sent a shudder of pleasure through her. 'I want to taste you,' he growled. 'Let me bite you. Feed me and I will show you untold ecstasy.'"

He laughed, tried to cover it with a cough, but she whacked him on the forehead with the paperback.

"You promised!" She tried to frown, but he could see the humor dancing in her eyes.

"Vampires? That's your kink, kitten?" Flipping over onto his front, he crawled toward her. "I vant to suck yoor blud," he lisped, burying his facing in her neck.

He nibbled the tender skin behind her ear, making her squirm and giggle some more. The sound of her laughter filled the room, sending his heart soaring. She should laugh every day. He had a new life mission.

"So, they're not real, then? Vampires, werewolves, things that go bump in the night?" He lifted his head, assuming she was still joking until he saw the serious question in her eyes. *What the hell?*

"Vampires? Have you been drinking the *Twilight* Kool-Aid, kitten?" He forced a laugh, wincing at the hollowness of it. *I'm fucking this up. She's just teasing, be cool.*

"Okay, no vamps. Is it just wolves, then, or are there other shifter types?"

The blood froze in his veins. "I don't know what you're talking about."

He'd planned to tell her. Would have done it the night she gave her statement to Jesse had Derek not warned him off. He hadn't needed words to warn Kirk; his tone of voice had spoken volumes. Losing himself in her body, it had been easier to pretend he was just a normal guy. Same as any other she'd met.

He turned his focus back to Silver. She didn't look scared, more curious, interested even. But what could he say? *Hey, baby, I'm a wolf.* He hesitated too long, sadness filled her expression, and she turned her face away.

"My mistake," she muttered.

Placing her book on the arm of the chair, Silver rose and moved toward the kitchenette. Disappointment tainted her scent, making his nose itch, driving the wolf inside him crazy. She was the one person in his life who believed in him, who smiled when he entered the room rather than looking for an escape route.

He couldn't stand it.

Vaulting over the back of the sofa, he stalked across the room, cornering her against the refrigerator. She kept her eyes averted, resisted his efforts to turn her face to him. Forcing her would leave a bruise on her delicate skin. Her hips might bear the imprint of his fingers, her left breast carried the outline of his teeth, but he would never cause her deliberate harm.

He dropped to his knees, curled his arms around her waist, and pressed his face into her belly. A strange sensation gnawed his gut, and he tried to place it. *Fear*. He was afraid. The scourge of the pack, the blunt-force trauma who held the line, providing the final point of defense was scared out of his mind.

"Talk to me," he begged.

"I thought this meant something to you. I thought we could be honest with each other." She kept her hands by her sides, not touching him.

He couldn't stand it. His Silver was tactile, petting, soothing, or stroking him whenever they were within touching distance.

"It does mean something; it means everything. You mean *everything*. Let me show you." He lifted her shirt. Pressing kisses to her torso, he fumbled with her top button.

"Stop it!" Her sharp cry stilled his hands. He slumped to the floor, at a loss at what to do next. He loved her, loved her so much, and he was fucking it up so badly.

"Tell me what to do, baby. Tell me what I need to do to make this right." His eyes burned, and he blinked hard.

She folded her hands around her middle, body

language closed in, defensive. "Be. Honest."

He opened his mouth, closed it again with a snap. He'd never been around anyone who wasn't like him. Not anyone who lived long enough for him to have to try and explain the otherness of his nature. He didn't know where to start. *I am a wolf. Four words, it's not fucking rocket science.* He didn't speak.

She shook her head, stepped around him, and opened the front door. *She can't leave, she can't!* He listened to the wood of the porch creak under her feet and waited for her to climb down the steps. His heart ached, a physical pain, as though it were tied to her by an invisible string, and she was ripping it from his body.

Her feet are bare!

He jumped up, flung himself through the door, clearing the steps in one bound. Sharp stones dug into the soles of his feet, but he didn't care. Too panicked to use his senses properly, he stared bewildered around the empty driveway. Wood creaked and he spun to find her standing on the porch. She pointed across the clearing.

"The wolf came from over there. I woke up and you were gone. I checked through the window when I couldn't find you, and this huge wolf came trotting out of the woods and stopped right there." She moved her arm to the exact spot where he'd shifted back to human. "There was a weird light, and then the wolf had vanished and you were there."

"Silver, baby, it's not what you think." Bullshit. It was exactly what she thought.

She ignored him. "I ran to the bathroom. I thought I must still be dreaming, and you acted like nothing happened. I tried to put it away, tried to convince myself I imagined it...."

"Silver—"

She held up her hand. "Think very carefully about the next words you say, Kirk."

He hated the way her body shook. Every protective instinct within him screamed to go to her, to gather her up in his arms and protect her. Turning his back, he paced away to the edge of the clearing. What to do, how to explain it? He wasn't a man of words; he was a man of action. *Show her.*

He strode toward the porch, uncaring of the stones pricking his feet. Stopping less than six feet from the steps, he stripped his clothing. The color rose on her cheeks, the way it always did when she saw his body. Ignoring his stiffening cock, Kirk reached for his wolf and shifted.

The miracle of what he was reflected in the wonderment in Silver's eyes. He kept the distance between them, turning in a slow circle to show her his wolf from every angle. Tilting his muzzle, he tested her scent for any sign of fear or disgust.

She moved to the edge of the porch and sat on the top step. Taking his cue, Kirk trotted over and rested his muzzle on her knees. Soft fingers brushed the fur between his ears, and the dread encapsulating his heart shattered. He raised his head, pressing into her hand, begging for a firmer touch. She scratched harder, digging her fingers into the thick ruff behind his head. His tongue lolled out, panting in ecstasy.

"You're beautiful," she breathed.

Turning his head, he licked her hand, and she giggled. He settled on his haunches, facing her. A frown creased between her eyes, and with a total lack of fear, she grabbed his muzzle, tilting his head to the side.

"Your scar is still there." Her fingers traced the white line, which neither fur nor the hair of his beard could cover.

Needing to touch her, to reassure himself of her acceptance, Kirk pushed back the wolf and resumed his human form. His muscles twitched in discomfort at shifting back and forth so rapidly, but he shook it off. One of the reasons he'd been chosen to protect the pack was his ability to handle multiple shifts in a short space of time.

Kneeling in the gravel, he stared up at her. "Tell me everything is okay between us," he pleaded.

She held out her hand to him. "Everything is okay."

Chapter Nine

Kirk held open the door of the diner for her, the expression on his face even grumpier than usual. She ducked beneath his arm and paused to take in the scene. It was a strange experience seeing the place open. A scattering of people occupied tables, including a small group of women. They turned toward the door with beaming smiles of welcome, easing the butterflies in her stomach. Having explained a little about the structure of the pack, it had been less of a surprise when Kirk told her he'd been summoned by Derek.

The alpha had decided to make some adjustments to Kirk's role in the pack. He played things close to the vest and was even more recalcitrant when it came to his past. He hadn't gone into detail, and she didn't press too hard. Things were still delicate between the two of them since he'd revealed his true nature. *The man I love can change into a wolf.* It blew her mind to think about it for too long.

The pack had a security company, and Derek wanted him to get involved in investigations. Jesse and Charlie were having problems running Razor to ground, and had asked The Defenders to check out some of the potential locations they'd been turning up as part of the investigation.

It had taken a direct order before Kirk would agree to leave Silver, even for a few hours. The alpha's mate and a few of the other female members of the pack had offered to keep her company and provide more insight into pack life. They'd chosen the diner because the sheer number of wolves present would alleviate his stress at not being there to protect her.

Although she loved every moment of their time together, she was glad of the break. His presence overwhelmed her, and Silver needed a little bit of breathing space to sort through her emotions. She loved Kirk; she knew that much at least. He acted like they were a permanent fixture, seeming to take it for granted that she would give up her whole life and integrate with his.

She'd been planning to leave her job in a few weeks anyway, so it wasn't like there was much to give up in all honesty. It was just the assumption that she would walk away without a second thought. He'd even been muttering about the search for Razor being a waste of time now the human world was no longer her concern.

Living with Kirk, loving him, that was the easy part. What bothered her was not knowing what she would do, what she could do to make a positive contribution to her new community. As traditional as her parents had been, they'd still raised her to be independent. To think for herself. To work to support herself. Kirk couldn't see the problem. If he had his way, she'd never leave the cabin. Would be barefoot and pregnant, keeping house and raising his kids. Kids? Puppies? *Oh God! What if she got pregnant and they came out furry?*

A gentle hand rested against her arm. "Talk to us, Silver. Something just freaked you the hell out. Tell us what you're worried about," Alexa urged.

Damn wolves and their super-noses.

"I was thinking about babies." She sighed. Two weeks and she was thinking about raising a family with a near stranger.

"Oh boy, you two would have the cutest pups." The woman next to Alexa sighed. Liana was a wolf, same as Alexa. The two women had mated humans— Jesse and Charlie, the two detectives who'd saved her life. In more ways than one.

By bringing her to Moonlight, they had introduced her to a world full of wonder. That hadn't been their intent, of course. But it didn't matter. In Kirk's arms, she understood the difference between living and existing. *So why am I looking for reasons not to embrace this new life?*

Liana's words sank in. "Pups? Like, four legs, wagging tail, cold nose pups?" Her hand fluttered over her stomach.

Alexa snorted. "You won't give birth to anything with fur. Is that what had you worried? I'm half-human. Any children you and Kirk may have in the future would be born in human form."

Alexa tilted her head. Kirk had the same mannerism, and now Silver knew the truth; she could identify a number of animalistic traits the wolves showed. "You love him?"

There was a hesitation, a question mark in

Alexa's tone, which made her uncomfortable. She bristled, wondering why she felt a need to defend her lover. "I do. Very much."

Whatever the other woman had been about to say got interrupted by the phone in her pocket. "Hi, Jesse. Yes, were still in the diner, just about to order something to eat. What's up?"

Silver lifted her menu. Browsing the lunch choices would give her a chance to calm her irritation. Kirk had his faults, sure, but the wary way the other members of the pack behaved around him pissed her off. Alexa tapped on the back of her menu, and she lowered it to find the other woman staring anxiously at her.

"There's a problem with your evidence. I don't know the full details, but the tape got damaged somehow. Talk to Jesse."

Taking the proffered phone, Silver lifted it to her ear. "Hello?"

"Hey, Silver. Damn, I'm so sorry, but someone screwed up here. Your evidence was submitted; Charlie and I checked the recording on the way to the station and it was fine. The clerk signed out the tape to transcribe it, and it's wiped."

A dull ache spread through her gut. It had taken everything she had to relive that night, and for nothing. "What does that mean for the case?"

Jesse sighed heavily in her ear. "Without your statement, we've got nothing. I'm sorry to ask, but could you come in and redo it?"

"Come in? As in to the station?" She bit her lip. Kirk would go ballistic if she left town without him. "Can it wait?"

"We're running the suspect down, Silver. We've

97

got everyone on it, including The Defenders. Charlie thinks we'll have him in custody today, so time is of the essence. Without any evidence, his lawyer will have him out within an hour of booking."

What to do? It was Kirk's first day in his new role, and scared as she might be, she couldn't expect him to come running and hold her hand. Hadn't Jesse just said they were close to catching Razor? "Okay. I'll do it."

"Great. That's great. I'm on my way to pick you up now. You'll be there and back before you know it." The phone went dead. She held it out to Alexa, trying to quell the nerves fluttering in her belly.

"Do you want us to come with you?" Riesa, the alpha's mate wrapped an arm around Silver's shoulder.

For a brief moment, she considered it. These four women were ready to do whatever she needed to feel safe. *Pack. This is what it means to be part of the pack.* Her doubts about the future melted away in the face of that realization. She had friends here; she just needed to give it time and settle in. They would help her to forge a place, to find a purpose.

She lifted her hand, squeezed Riesa's fingers where they held her, and smiled. "I'll be fine. Jesse and Charlie will be there to look after me."

Riesa opened her mouth, paused for a moment, then shook her head. "I'm sure they will take good care of you. Just promise me one thing. Tell Kirk where you are going. He needs to feel in control of things." She removed her arm from Silver's back and tapped her menu. "You need to eat. I really want a burger, but I'm going with the chicken salad. I wish I had a wolf's metabolism."

"Salad sounds good," Silver agreed. "And maybe just a tiny slice of pie."

The tension around the table relaxed into laughter and appreciative coos over the Moonlight Diner's legendary key lime pie. She knew Riesa was right, but that didn't mean she was looking forward to Kirk's reaction. *I'll call him from the station.*

***

Jesse tried to be reassuring, but the more he told her there would be no problem, the more nervous she felt. He pulled the truck into the parking lot at the back of the station and led her through a security entrance. Showing her to a shabby-looking waiting room, he patted her arm.

"I'll just check on Charlie, darlin', make sure everything is set up for your statement."

She perched on the edge of the dark-green couch and dug in her purse for the disposable phone Kirk had given her. He'd programmed in his number. Taking a deep breath, she connected the call. The nervous feeling in her stomach increased with every chirp of the ring tone in her ear. *Pick up, pick up.*

"Leave a message," his gruff voice said, followed by a sharp beep.

"Oh, um...hey, Kirk, it's Silver. I'm fine, everything is fine, so don't get mad when you pick this up. There was a problem with my statement, so I'm at the station with Jesse and Charlie to do another one."

She paused, checking the clock on the wall. "It's a quarter after one. I shouldn't be more than an hour. Maybe you could come and pick me up? I have to go.

Love you."

Swallowing down the lump in her throat, she forced a smile she didn't feel as Jesse stuck his head around the door. "Ready to start?"

The station was busy. People hunched over computers, talking into phones, shouting information to each other across the room Jesse led her through. She ducked her head down. After the peace and quiet of the cabin, the hubbub unsettled her.

It was a relief when they entered the interview room, leaving the noise behind them.

"Hey, Silver." Charlie grinned at her, his long dark hair tied off his face in a tight cue at the nape of his neck. "Take a seat."

She sat on the opposite side of the scarred table, huddled against the wall. *You're being foolish. You're in a building surrounded by cops; there's nothing to be afraid of.* She sat straighter in her seat, ignoring the urge to check her phone. She hadn't anticipated Kirk wouldn't answer when she called. *He's busy.*

A knock on the door interrupted the train wreck of her thoughts, and she turned toward it. An overweight man filled the open doorway, sweat beading on his forehead and darkening the pale-blue shirt he wore beneath the arms. The smile on his face didn't reach his eyes. She glanced at Charlie, then Jesse. They both looked pissed at the interruption.

"Ray."

"Hey, guys, sorry to bust in, but I thought you'd want to be in on it. I've been pressing my informants, and I've got a solid lead on Razor. I know it's your case, so figured you'd want to be the ones to take him." He pulled a handkerchief from his pocket. "Damn this heat."

The detectives went on point, their attention all on their colleague. Jesse checked the gun on his hip. "You're sure the information is solid?"

"Absolutely. My guy hasn't let me down yet. Your suspect is holed up in an empty apartment on Cherry."

"I know the place," Charlie said, eyes shining with excitement. "It's on the list I drew up of possible hideout locations."

The men were halfway out the door before they stopped. "Shit, Silver. I'm sorry," Jesse said.

She could see the conflict in his face. His need to do his job, to catch the killer. That's what they all wanted, right?

"It's okay. I can wait. If you catch him, then you will need my evidence straight away. I called Kirk and let him know where I was, so he should be here soon."

"Hey, Jesse. I can keep an eye on, Silver is it?" Ray said. "You hungry, sweetheart?"

She shook her head. "I could do with a coffee, though."

"Great. No problem. I'll take you to the break room and get you one."

Jesse hesitated still.

She gave him a smile, making a shooing motion with her hand. "Go. Catch the bad guy. The sooner he's in custody, the sooner things can get back to normal."

With a nod of thanks, he was gone, leaving her alone with Ray. He flashed her that insincere smile again. Suppressing a shudder of dislike, she allowed him to usher her into the corridor.

"It's just up ahead, on the right." He nudged her

in front of him, and she moved forward. "Here."

Silver stared in confusion at the thick steel door. "It's the emergency exit." Something hard dug into the small of her back.

"Don't do anything stupid, bitch. I've been looking for you for a fucking week." He jabbed her again. "Hurry up before somebody sees us."

Oh, God. I'm sorry, Kirk. She gripped the push bar in her shaking hands and opened the door. Ray grabbed her shoulder, forcing her down the stairs and out into the parking lot.

"Over there. The blue sedan. Don't try anything stupid now."

The muzzle of his gun poked her again, catching between two of her ribs. Pain drove the breath from her lungs, and she staggered forward. He forced her into the car, rounded the hood with the gun tucked against his side. He climbed in, the tortured shock absorbers doing little to cushion his weight. The car sank lower on his side.

"What are you doing? Jesse and Charlie will be back soon. How long do you think it will take them to put two and two together?" She tried to keep her voice calm. If she could reason with him, maybe he would change his mind. "If you take me back inside, I won't say anything. I promise."

The engine started, and he steered one-handed out of the lot, keeping the gun trained on her. "You think I'm stupid? Those two glory hounds won't be coming back. They're going to get more than they bargained for."

Stomach clenching, she leaned her head against the window as she absorbed the enormity of the situation. Jesse and Charlie were heading for a trap.

This wasn't a spur-of-the-moment thing. They'd planned this. Whoever they were.

She turned her head to look at him. "Why are you doing this?" she whispered.

"I needed the cash. The taskforce is fucking everything up, disrupting the gangs, and cutting off my income streams. When they turned your tape in last week, I saw my chance. I gave your details to Razor, but you'd disappeared."

He glanced at her. The dark circles under his arms were spreading. The sour odor of his sweat filled the car, making her want to heave. He flicked his eyes back to the road, took a left turn, and risked another quick look at her. Fear widened his eyes. She recognized the look, had seen it on her own face too often those first couple of days after the murder.

"He's not someone you want to be on the wrong side of, girl. I had to do something to draw you out, so I wiped the tape. Set things up with the gang, told them to be ready."

They passed through a quiet neighborhood, turned again, and the number of houses lessened giving way to a more industrial landscape. She didn't recognize the area at all. The few months she'd been in Florida, she'd stuck close to home. Everything she needed had been within a handful of blocks. Her original plan had been to spend the summer exploring, and then it didn't seem worth bothering to go farther afield once she'd decided to leave town.

Ray cut down a narrow road between two large buildings and pulled up around the back next to a loading dock. The paint on the doors had split and peeled. The high windows of the warehouse were either broken or boarded up.

"Get out."

His voice made her jump, and she fumbled with the lock of her seatbelt. He climbed out of the car, waving the gun toward the large double-doors. She edged around the rear of the vehicle and winced when he grabbed her arm, dragging her across the cracked concrete. He rapped on the door with the butt of the gun, looking over his shoulder ever couple of seconds.

"Come on, come on." His fat cheeks glistened with sweat, his shirt practically soaked through. *He's not as sure about this plan as he's making out.*

It might be sheer bravado on her part, but Silver seized on the tiny thread of hope. Jesse and Charlie were smart guys; maybe they would get out okay. And then there was Kirk. Kirk would find her. He'd tear the world apart to get to her, she just needed to hang on, not do anything stupid.

The door swung open, and Ray shoved her forward. She stumbled, blinded for a moment by the contrast between the dark interior and the bright sunshine outside. Hard hands grabbed her arms, pinning them behind her back. Fear surged, sending her heart racing.

She couldn't let it take hold, had to keep calm, stay focused. Stay alive as long as she could. *My name is Silver Ellis. I live in the town of Moonlight. Kirk Matheson is my mate. He will come for me.* She repeated the litany in her mind, slowing her breathing.

The shadows within the warehouse resolved themselves. A pile of trash in the corner gave the impression someone had made an attempt at cleaning up. Wooden crates cluttered the space, their tops ripped open, contents spilled on the floor. She risked a look at the man holding her arms. The boyishness of his face surprised her. He was just a kid, seventeen, eighteen at best.

"Hi, my name is Silver." She gave him a tentative smile.

"Shut up, bitch." He shook her arm, and she lowered her eyes immediately.

Ray looked around the warehouse. "Where the fuck is Razor? I need to get out of here before anyone notices I'm missing from the station."

"Chill, fat man. He'll be here soon." An older, rougher-looking man stepped forward. He chucked an envelope at Ray. "There's your money. Now get the fuck outta here."

The detective caught the envelope, glanced once at Silver, then turned away. "Pleasure doing business," he called over his shoulder.

A third man closed the warehouse door, sliding a thick bar into place to secure it. He didn't even glance her way as he walked past, heading toward a group of old chairs that looked like they'd been rescued from the local dump. The money man studied her, clicked his tongue behind his teeth, and shook his head.

"You've caused us way too much trouble, bitch. If I had it my way, you'd be dead already." The hard look on his face told her he spoke the absolute truth. He would kill her and not think twice about it. She shrank back against the younger man holding her.

Money-man bared his teeth in a mockery of a smile. "Razor is a vindictive bastard. He wants the pleasure of bleeding you out himself." He looked past her to the man holding her captive. "Take her over there. Tie her up."

Come on, Kirk. Find me.

Chapter Ten

Kirk stood among the ruins of Silver's living room. He'd called in to collect a few more things while he was in the area, wanting to surprise her. Found her home violated. The guts of her cozy furniture lay spilled out over the floor, her television smashed. Books shredded and defaced. Obscene threats were scrawled across the walls. The bedroom looked worse. The devastation before him was personal, not the product of punks looking for things to steal. Her clothing had been slashed, her bed used as a toilet.

Rage built within him. Expanded with every beat of his heart until there was nothing human left. He was death. He was vengeance. Whoever had done this would not survive to see the sunrise. The phone in his pocket chirped. He pulled it out and stared at the screen. *Silver*. He tucked it away. He couldn't speak to her, not right now.

He'd go to her tonight, with the blood of her enemies hot on his tongue. Show her his true nature and hope she could accept him. He might be enough of a bastard that he wouldn't let her go even if she couldn't, but she needed to know the truth. The man she thought she loved was a sham. Kirk Matheson was the devil in human form.

Time to get to work.

Glass crunched beneath his feet. He crouched, tugged a crumpled photograph from the shattered frame he'd stepped on. A much younger Silver stared shyly from the picture, bracketed by an older, smiling couple. He straightened the corner carefully and tucked the photo away in the inside pocket of his leather jacket. Without a backward glance, he walked away from one scene of destruction, hell-bent on creating another.

He threw himself into the driver's seat of his truck and grabbed the notebook from the dash. There were a couple of locations left on his list to check—an apartment block in a rundown part of town and a warehouse to the north. Charlie had been busy digging into the gang's background and had drawn up a list of potential hideouts. Derek had divided up the list; he and Rand were checking the other possibilities.

Corralling his fury, Kirk retrieved his phone to call the alpha. If the others had already tracked down the gang, he needed to move fast. He didn't have any beef with Jesse or Charlie, but they wouldn't be allowed to stand in the way. Silver belonged to the pack now, and Kirk delivered justice for the pack.

The message icon flashed on the screen. His determination waivered for a moment. He longed to hear his mate's sweet voice, but he couldn't risk it. She was a weakness he couldn't afford to indulge right now. He dialed Derek's number instead.

"Hey, Kirk. That garage was a bust. Rand's not

having any luck either. Did you get what you needed from Silver's place?"

Good, they haven't found them yet. "It's trashed. They know who she is." Saying the words aloud brought clarity. A snarl ripped from his throat. "They fucking know who she is. Someone betrayed us." Silence from the other end of the line raised his hackles. "What's going on?" he snapped.

"Didn't Silver call you? She promised Riesa she would call you on the way to the station."

Ice filled his veins. The hot fury he'd been battling to control turned to ashes. "Tell me what the fuck you're talking about." He could barely hear the words of explanation from his alpha over the roar of blood pumping through his veins. With a couple of massive leaps, he cleared the flights of steps from her apartment to the ground floor. He slammed through the communal door and raced for his vehicle.

The journey from Silver's apartment to the police station passed in a blur. He pressed the message replay on his phone again. "Oh, um...hey, Kirk, it's Silver. I'm fine, everything is fine...." Her gentle voice filled the cab of his truck, lashing his soul. Screeching to a halt outside the station, he barreled through the door, sending a young uniformed officer flying.

"Where is she?" he yelled, stepping over the kid's legs to brace his hands on the front counter.

"I need you to calm down, sir," the clerk stammered.

"Where is Silver Ellis? I need to see her right now." Fucking humans were too stupid for their own good. It amazed him they had survived to be the dominant species on the planet when they couldn't recognize a predator among them.

The clerk's face paled, and he backed away from the desk.

"It's okay, Mike. We've got this."

Kirk swung toward the familiar voice, the other humans in the room forgotten. "Where is she, Jesse?" The man's disheveled appearance registered. "What the fuck happened to you?"

A livid bruise decorated the detective's left cheek, and his filthy clothes were ripped in places. Charlie hadn't faired any better, given the way he cradled his wrist.

Jesse limped toward a door marked *Authorized Personnel Only.* "Come on, she's in the break room. I'll fill you in on the way."

Kirk tried to focus on their story about a tip-off on Razor's location, the late realization it was a trap, and the ensuing gun fight. A couple of punks, junior members of the gang eager to earn their stripes. Dead now. The apartment on Cherry had been one of the two locations remaining on his list.

"But no sign of Razor?" He needed to be clear on that. Needed to know his target was still out there.

Jesse shook his head, using his shoulder to push open the door of the break room. "Nah, man, just a couple of kids." He looked sickened over having killed the young men. *Weak.* Kirk didn't have time for weakness. He needed to get Silver to a safe place, and then the whole gang was dead.

Every last one of them.

Shoving past Jesse, he ground to a halt in the empty room and drew a deep breath. No honeysuckle. He turned on Jesse with a growl, grabbing a fistful of his filthy shirt. "What the fuck kind of game are you playing, Farrell? Silver's never been in here."

"Easy, Kirk. Take it easy. Let me call Ray and find out where they are," Charlie cut in.

"Ray? Who the fuck is Ray?" He shoved Jesse out of the way and stormed into the corridor.

Tracking back and forth, he sorted the myriad of scents clogging the passageway. *Focus, focus. There!* The delicate beauty of her unique fragrance called to him. Sprinting down the corridor, he slammed his shoulder against a heavy steel door, stumbling down the first few steps in his hurry. He ran out into the parking lot, stopped, and turned in a slow circle, trying to pick up the trail.

Engine oil, gas fumes, a hint of rubber. She'd transferred into a vehicle on this spot, by choice or force, he couldn't tell. The two detectives reached him, Jesse still limping. The ice coating his veins cracked, the ravenous fury boiling forth like a volcanic eruption. Claws burst from his fingers, and his jaw stretched wide to accommodate his fangs.

"Fuck, Kirk! Hold it together, man," Charlie yelled. "You can't shift here!"

The human was right. He needed more information before he could unleash the wolf. *Soon, brother. Soon we will bathe in blood and vengeance.* He sucked in a breath and shackled the beast inside.

"That's it. That's better. Take a minute and we can figure this out." Charlie lowered his voice, raised a hand to pat Kirk on the arm, and decided better of it. Good call on his part. He had information they didn't. He needed to share what he knew, use them to aid in the search for Razor.

"The gang knows about Silver. I went by her place earlier. It's a wreck." A red film washed over his vision, and he clenched his fists until his knuckles turned white. "They wrote stuff on the walls. Threats. They know who she is. There's a leak somewhere, and it's not in the pack."

"Ray!" Jesse shook his head. "He's the one who gave us the bogus tip, that asshole!" Another name to add to the list. Cop or no cop, Ray would die.

Charlie lowered his phone. "No answer from him. Where the hell is he?" He glanced around the lot. "His car's gone. Hold on a minute." He lifted his phone again, spoke to a colleague, and requested a trace on Ray's service vehicle. "Northside? The industrial park, yeah I know it. Hey! Kirk, where are you going?" Charlie yelled across the lot after him.

He paused, turned, and snarled. "I know where she is. Don't follow me."

"Come on now, you know we can't let you do this," Jesse said, hobbling toward him.

The leash on Kirk's temper snapped. "Time to fucking choose, Jesse. This is pack business, now. *My* business. Your laws don't count when it comes to one of our own. If you can't back me up, then stay the fuck out of my way."

Kirk gave the wolf inside him its head, using the animal's strength to give him extra speed. He rounded the building, jumped into his truck, and roared away from the curb. A piece of paper fluttered beneath the windscreen wiper, but he ignored it. If he survived the next couple of hours, a parking ticket would be the least of his worries.

I'm coming, Silver. Hold on for me, baby. I'm coming.

***

Shards of wood flew in every direction as the wolf threw his weight against the warehouse door. Landing on four paws, he shook the splinters free, his fur too thick for any to penetrate to the skin below. Shouts and curses greeted his arrival, followed swiftly by a volley of gunfire. The bullets thunked harmlessly into the concrete behind him as the wolf sprinted for the shadowy edges of the room.

He lifted his head and loosed an eerie howl that echoed around the cavernous space. The delicious scent of fear drifted to his nose. Humans might not live among the wolves now, but their DNA carried the imprint of their ancestors. Their limbic system recognized a deadly threat stalked them.

Darting left, he evaded another flurry of shots, hunkered low, and crawled toward his first target. The man peered around the corner of a pile of packing cases, staring at the spot where Kirk had been. He leapt on the man's back, using his claws to rake down his sides, spilling blood and other, thicker things. Screams rent the air, and he sprinted away without making a killing strike. The noise of the dying man would add to the confusion.

Finding a spot that would shield him from view, Kirk pushed back the wolf and resumed his human form. He needed to analyze the layout of the warehouse, pinpoint Silver's location, and catalog the numbers he faced. Ignoring the screams, he studied the ill-lit room. His best-case scenario of facing a handful of the gang went out the window. Using sight and smell, he identified at least twenty individual scents, and, *thank fuck!* the sweet, delicate aroma of honeysuckle.

"Silver!"

"I'm here, Kirk, I'm okay—" His beloved mate's voice ended in a cry of pain and a crack of flesh against flesh.

"Shut up, bitch! Hey, whoever the fuck you are, you're a dead man. No one attacks the Lobos and lives to talk about it."

Kirk threw back his head and laughed. The audacity of these worthless little shits to label themselves as wolves. Time to teach them the error of their ways. Time to show them what a real wolf was capable of. He pushed to his feet, heedless of his nudity, and strode into one of the thin beams cast by the overhead lighting.

"Whoa! Look at the size of him."

"What the fuck, man? Why you naked?"

The questions and nervous laughter flew from the main group as he stalked toward them. His lack of visible weapons made them cocky. The braggadocious nature they wore as part of their gang culture forcing them into stupidity.

No gun, no threat.

He kept his pace steady, waiting for the right moment. A couple of shoulders dropped, one of the younger kids turned to the others, grabbing his crotch and making a dirty comment. Laughter. *Perfect.*

He transitioned from walking to running too fast for the human eye. Traveling at full speed, he called the wolf, landing in the center of the group in a slash of claws and teeth. Blood flew. Bones crunched between his jaws. Flesh parted as he struck and sliced his way through them. Heat flashed along his left flank, a sharper pain stabbed his shoulder, but he shook it off. No time to catalogue his hurts, not when there was so much death to be delivered.

The floor of the warehouse grew slippery beneath his paws, the blood of his victims combining with that flowing from his wounds. His front right leg wouldn't take his weight, and he stumbled. A loud report echoed close to his head, and fire lanced down his spine. With a shout of pain, Kirk shifted to human form, threw himself at the man who had just shot him, and smashed his jaw with a meaty punch.

The shift helped with some of the injuries, but there were too many for his shifter ability to handle. His right hand hung at an odd angle, so he smashed his elbow into the nose of the nearest attacker. Silver was close, he could scent her, even through the blood, sweat, and pain that surrounded him. Bodies littered the floor, but they kept coming. He needed to shift.

Another bullet struck him in the lower back, and he collapsed to one knee. *Failed. I've failed my mate, my pack.* He pushed to his feet, grabbed the young man who ran at him, wrenched his head, and dropped the corpse on the floor.

"Motherfucker! I'm gonna kill you, I'm gonna slice your guts open and watch you bleed to death," a voice screamed. He turned to see a man with a livid scar down his cheek—Razor. He recognized him from the description Silver gave during her witness statement.

Kirk smiled. He wasn't going to make it out alive. The damage to his body told him that, but he'd take the gang leader with him. He raised his left hand and beckoned to the human. A blow struck his shoulder, spinning him around, knocking him to the floor. He tried to lift himself up but fell back again. Razor stood over him, a glint of madness in his eyes. The man crouched over him, a knife glinting in his right hand. He raised his arm to deliver the killing blow.

With the last of his energy, Kirk struck, sinking his claws into Razor's throat. Hot blood poured from the ruined flesh, splashing across his face. The dead gang leader toppled sideways, pinning him to the cold concrete floor.

A chorus of howls split the air, and Kirk blinked hard, trying to focus on the wavering image above him. He must be hallucinating. Or perhaps his ancestors had come to take him to their final resting place. His eyelids felt like lead weights. He gave into the urge to close them, just for a moment. *No. Can't give up, Silver needs me.* The heavy weight across his chest shifted, allowing him to draw a shallow breath.

He forced his eyes open and stared in wonder at the image of his mate's beautiful face floating before him. Snarls, screams, and howls rent the air around them, the familiar scents of the pack drifted over him. "I'm sorry, I couldn't save you, baby," he whispered.

Soft hands stroked his face, a soothing balm against the pain radiating through every part of his body. "You came for me, Kirk. I knew you would."

"I'll always come for you, kitten." His voice rasped in his ears. He coughed, a wet ugly sound.

"I know. I know." She laid her head against his cheek, her tears soaking into his beard. His Silver was crying. She shouldn't ever cry; he'd sworn to make her laugh. He tried to lift his arm, to cradle her head, but he couldn't move.

A shadow fell across his face. He blinked away the tears in his eyes and stared into the golden eyes of his alpha. Strong fingers cupped the side of his face.

"Rest now, my brother. It's done. Your mate is safe from harm, and I will protect her with my own life. Sleep easy."

The blackness swallowed him whole.

Epilogue

Kirk set his computer to one side as the sweet scent of his mate filled the room. She paused on the threshold of the bedroom, her delectable curves hidden beneath a shapeless cotton dress.

"You're supposed to be resting."

He growled deep in his chest. "I'm bored of fucking resting. I've been stuck in this bed for a week now." A sly smile played about his mouth. "If you came over here and laid down beside me, I'm sure I could manage to rest some more."

The musical chime of her laughter rang out. "Kirk Matheson, I know all about your idea of *resting*."

With an aggrieved sigh, he tried to settle himself more comfortably against the pile of pillows at his back. He winced, and she flew across the room like a shot.

"What is it, what hurts?" She cupped his rough-bearded cheek, eyes full of concern.

Grabbing her hand, he dragged it under the covers and curled her fingers around the throbbing length of his cock. "This, baby. It hurts real bad. Maybe a cramp or something?"

The pupils in her chocolate-brown eyes expanded; the deep-rose flush he loved so much bloomed on her cheek. Her breathing faltered, and the delicate fragrance of her arousal perfumed the air. Her hand shaped his flesh, slid to the bottom of his shaft, and back up to massage the flared head in her palm.

"I missed you, kitten," he moaned.

"We shouldn't," she whispered, though she kept working his cock. "The healer said you almost died."

Soft tears glistened on the tips of her lashes, shredding his heart. He grabbed her by the waist, hauling her onto his lap. Arms wrapped tight around her, he rocked back and forth while she cried.

"I'm sorry," she gasped. "I don't mean to be silly. It's just.... Oh, Kirk, I was so scared I would lose you."

He cupped the back of her head, pressing her face into the curve of his neck. "Hush, kitten. Hush now, I'm here. I'm right here, and I'm never going to let you out of my sight again."

The storm of weeping passed soon enough. He understood it to be more relief than anything else, his mate letting go the tension now she knew he was going to be okay. He'd choked back a few sobs of his own after waking up safe in their bed a couple of nights ago. Her tears dried against his skin. She brushed a kiss beneath his ear, and the soothing strokes he made against her back shifted to something harder, more urgent. He slid his hands lower, cupping her plump ass, loving the way she filled his hands to overflowing.

A guttural moan escaped her lips. "You need to

rest."

"I need to fuck you." He snarled in frustration at the voluminous folds of material trapped between their bodies. "I need you out of this dress, baby."

She wriggled away from his hold, regained her feet beside the bed, and toyed with the buttons running down the bodice. He lowered his eyebrows in a frown, too impatient for games.

"Don't test me, kitten."

"Oh, hush yourself." She gave him a cheeky grin, unfastening her dress to the waist. Trailing one finger down her sternum, she parted the ugly cotton to reveal a silk cream teddy, edged in lace. He leaned forward, tried to grab her wrist, but she danced out of reach.

"Show me the rest," he demanded.

With a twist of her hips, she removed the rest of her dress, leaving it to pool at her feet. Grasping the edge of the sheet, she tugged it down his body, baring his straining cock to her greedy gaze. She bent forward, the thick waves of her hair cascading into his lap as she stretched her lips wide and swallowed the head of his cock.

The heat of her mouth scalded his aching flesh, and he buried his hands in her hair, using the silken strands to distract him from thrusting his hips. Her hand clenched on his thigh. She pulled back, slid forward again, and took him deeper. There was more enthusiasm than skill to her technique, but he didn't much care when she used the tip of her tongue to probe the perfect spot just beneath the head.

Being a passive participant didn't come naturally to him, and the smell of her arousal was driving him crazy. He clutched her hips, lifting and turning her body at the same time until she sprawled across his chest, her pussy mere inches from his face. The pale silk covering her sex was soaked with her cream. Lifting his head, he sucked the material into his mouth, drawing on the taste he craved.

She moaned around his cock, taking him deeper in response to the brush of his mouth. He released the snaps on the teddy, and dove forward to shove his tongue as deep into her core as he could. He fucked her hard and fast, fingers convulsing around her hips.

He'd come so close to losing her, to losing everything, including his life. The need to prove they'd cheated death stirred deep within him. Raising his hand, he smacked his palm hard against the left cheek of her ass. She released his cock with a sharp cry, turning her head to stare in disbelief at him over one shoulder.

"I told you what would happen if you disobeyed me, kitten," he snarled. Fastening his mouth on her clit, he teased the tender bundle of nerves and slapped her ass again, striking the same spot.

"Kirk!"

He smoothed his hand over the red mark, warming and soothing her abused flesh. Flattening his tongue, he massaged her clit in time with the motion of his hand. His name on her lips became a moan of pleasure. She rocked against his face, seeking her pleasure, and he couldn't keep a grin from his face. There was no shyness left in his mate; she knew what she needed and went after it. It was time to raise the stakes. He dropped his head back against the pillows, ignoring her grumbles at losing contact with his mouth.

"Turn for me, baby. I need to be inside this hot

little pussy of yours," he ordered, lifting and helping her to maneuver as he spoke.

As eager as him, she no sooner found her balance before she pressed back, guiding his cock inside the blazing-hot heaven of her sex. He raised his hips, shoving up to meet her downward thrust, impaling her to the hilt with a shout of satisfaction.

"You're mine, baby. Don't you forget it." He slammed upward again, sending her sprawling over his chest.

"Yours, Kirk. Always," she panted.

Nails digging into his shoulders, she scrabbled for purchase, found it, and rammed her hips back to meet his. Their flesh slapped together, the desperate thrusts punctuated by gasps and grunts of exertion. Bodies moving in a dance as old as time, they came together again and again.

Heat built inside him, drawing his balls up tight against his body, warning him he was close. He thrust his hand between them, trapped her clit between thumb and finger, and pinched hard. "Come for me, Silver. Come for me now, baby."

She fell over the edge of bliss. He caught her. He would always catch her. Holding her close, he pumped his hips, filling her body with his seed, marking her, claiming her, owning her. *Mate, my mate.*

A car door slammed, distracting Kirk, and he grabbed Silver by the hips, holding her still. "Someone's here."

Lifting her head from his chest, she pushed the sweaty strands of her hair from her face. "Oh, that's just the first of the pack arriving."

With a soft moan, she separated their bodies and

climbed from the bed. He should probably close his mouth at some point, but her nonchalant words were struggling to register.

"What are you talking about? They know the rules. No one comes here."

"Well, they do now. I had plenty of time to think about your rules, you know, when you were practically dead." She planted her hands on her hips, glaring down at him. "I've made some new rules, and we're having a party to celebrate."

"A party?" *What the fuck happened in the last week?*

"They came to help us, Kirk. Every last one of them. From the alpha to the omega. They came to the warehouse and fought the gang. We needed them, and they saved us, so the least we can do is say thank you. Now, stop growling and get that sexy ass of yours in the shower." She turned on her heel, leaving him stunned.

My kitten has claws, and it's hot as fuck.

***

Kirk surveyed the noisy group invading his space. A row of parked vehicles stretched along the access road. Chairs and tables scattered the edges of the clearing, making the most of the shade from the overhanging trees. Alan and Shelley from the diner had set up a couple of grills and were busy flipping burgers and grilling chicken. Tables next to them groaned beneath the weight of side dishes other pack members had brought with them.

He'd expected to feel awkward, a fish out of water. The proverbial bull in the china shop of their fragile, precious pack. Silver had other ideas, however. It was clear that in the week he'd been out of action, she'd established herself in the hearts of the pack. The handshakes and hugs he'd received had been tentative, but no less heartfelt than the more demonstrative embraces she'd been swept into.

The alpha smiled down at his mate and pressed a kiss to her forehead. Separating himself from the group surrounding Silver, he made his way to where Kirk leaned against the side of the cabin. His attempts at hiding from the party had proven an utter failure. One member of the pack after the other invaded his self-imposed isolation.

His mind still reeled from their words. Everyone had a story to share with him, a memory, something Kirk had done that directly affected them. Every sin he had committed, every death delivered had been flipped on its head as they thanked him for a mate who'd been saved, for an escape hard won. Far from the devil he painted himself, they saw him as a savior.

Taking the beer Derek offered to him, Kirk chugged half of it down. The alpha propped his shoulder against the wall, crossed his feet at the ankles, and surveyed his pack.

"They didn't stay away because they feared you, Kirk. They stayed away because of the guilt they carried."

"Guilt? About what?"

"You took the strain. You shielded them from the worst of the horrors we faced, and they let you do it. *I* let you do it."

Kirk stared across the clearing toward his mate. She threw her head back, the bright cadence of her laughter floating through the air. As though sensing his eyes upon her, she turned her head and met his gaze. Love shone in her eyes. No fear, no doubt, only love and acceptance.

His heart soared. Basking in her love, the broken pieces of his soul began to knit together.

"She's a remarkable young woman," Derek said.

Kirk lifted his beer, clinking his bottle against the alpha's. "You have no idea." *Nor do I, but I can't wait to find out.* He held out his hand to Silver, unable to hide a grin of pride when she abandoned the group mid-sentence to come to him.

"I have something I want to show you," he said, curling a possessive arm around her waist.

"You need to get some new material, buster. Don't think that just because we're mated you won't have to work for it." Laughter danced in her eyes, and he swooped down on her to press a kiss to her lips.

He lost himself in the sweet temptation of her mouth, until the chorus of catcalls and hoots from the rest of the pack grew to a deafening volume. Flipping them the bird behind his back, he led his mate inside. He tugged her onto his knee, opened his laptop, and called up the plans for his new project. Silver studied the screen, a sweet frown of concentration on her face. *Work it out, kitten.*

She looked up at him, cupping his cheek to make sure she had his full attention. "Is this for me?" she breathed.

He nodded. "I wanted to make sure you could keep doing what you love. It will take a while to construct, but with your own space you can set up a virtual classroom. Alexa is a whiz online. She'll be able to help you with a website. A lot of the others work in the virtual world, too. I'm going to take a couple of classes, learn about the right kind of setup for you—"

She silenced him with a kiss. "It's amazing. I love it. I love you. Thank you for helping me to find my place in the world."

About the Author

Merryn Dexter is a military spouse who, after a varied employment career (from selling sandals to old ladies with bunions to being a health and safety coordinator for a construction company), is thrilled to be pursuing her dream career as a romance writer. She likes The Winchesters, Spike, Hotch, Loki and watching complicated European Noir. Her hobbies include crying at books, crying at movies, crying at tv serials (there's a theme!) and believes all stories should have a Happy Ending.

Also by Merryn Dexter

www.ingramcontent.com/pod-product-compliance
Lightning Source LLC
Chambersburg PA
CBHW070338130626
46556CB00007B/2927